Unfettered
Omega

S. Rodman

Dark Angst Publishing

This book contains,

Dubious consent

On page depiction of rape that is heard from the next room. And then the immediate aftermath is dealt with.

Captivity/ Slavery

Depression

Physical abuse

Reference to cot death

On page murder of a baddie

Blurb

Is he here to save me? Or is he just another captor?

I'm a slave. Nothing more than property. The very thing I never wanted to be, and the very reason I ran away from my pack.

Seems like fate has a cruel sense of humor.

Being enslaved in a harem, even a billionaire's, is no life at all.

'Ritchie's Rainbow', they call us. Each of us are named and dressed in a different color. Red, Blue, Jade, Gray, Pink, Yellow and Indigo. I've been called Red for so long, I can barely remember my real name.

A vampire, siren, fey, demon, vessel, kelpie and me, a wolf shifter. All imprisoned for the pleasure of a wealthy human, to use for himself and to lend to his friends.

I take care of the other boys the best I can, they are brothers to me and it's in my omega nature to be nurturing. But it is hard when we are all suffering so much.

But Brodie, the new healer, seems kind under his gruff exterior.

I see something in his eyes. Something that gives me hope.

I think he might just be here to save us all.

But I don't think falling for me is part of the plan.

Am I going to ruin everything?

Or will I finally find freedom? Finally become unfettered?

Character List

Red – Red is a wolf shifter omega

Brodie – Is a human and a healer (A doctor who knows how to take care of all the different paranormal beings)

Lello / Yellow – Is a Kelpie, a shape shifting water horse from Scotland.

Ned / Indigo – Is a young vampire. If he hadn't been turned in his twenties he would be 98 years old.

Blue – Is a siren. He is not allowed to talk or sing encase he enchants everyone with his voice.

Gray – Is a type of demon called an Incubus, he feeds on sex, but he has been imprisoned for so long he no longer enjoys it.

Pink – Is a vessel, a human who absorbs magic from the world around them, but cannot wield it. Vessels need to be emptied of the magic they have accumulated by having sex with a mage.

Jade – Is part fey. The fey realm used to be close to the human one, enabling fey to cross over, but the realms drifted apart and it is no longer possible to cross over. A sect called Revivalist search for humans with strong fey ancestry and breed them in an attempt to strengthen the bloodline.

Contents

Chapter One

Brodie

I've only reached the lobby and I'm feeling out of my depth. It's a veritable sea of white marble. A floor that stretches out forever to create a vast empty space of sheer opulence lined by giant windows. There is more wealth in the lobby of this skyscraper than I will ever have in my lifetime. By the magnitude of a few thousand.

My mind is struggling to comprehend it. This is the very center of London, where every inch of land comes with a price tag that includes more zeros than I've had hot dinners. Trying to grasp the sheer amount of wealth that I am looking at, is blowing my mind. And this is just the entrance.

I'm headed for the penthouse. Thirty floors of luxury apartments belonging to Saudi princes, Russian Oligarchs and Chinese tech firm owners and above them all, figuratively and literally, the penthouse of Richard Smithson. Billionaire and fourth richest man on the planet. Beaten only by Bill Gates, Jeff Bezos and Elon Musk.

I've never felt more daunted in my life. I'm I really up to the task? Do I have what it takes? Right now, I'm not sure that I do.

Sounds of shouting catch my attention and distract me from my doubts. The noise is coming from what looks like the discreet door to what I guess is the stairwell. There is no part of my nature that will let me ignore whatever is going on, so I make my way over.

To my surprise, the stairwell is nearly as lavish as the lobby. I'd been expecting bare concrete. Surely the residents never use the stairs? They must use the gaudy glass and gold lifts? Stairs in fancy buildings are usually only for staff and deliveries.

My musing is disrupted by the clatter of running feet. Many pairs of feet, all running down the stairs towards me. Gruff voices, sounding very out of breath bellow "Stop!" This is the shouting I heard.

I glance up, just in time to see someone vault the railings and drop straight down to where I am standing. What the hell are they thinking? That is far too high to jump from. I step forward and catch them in my arms.

They land with a force that makes me stagger as well as knocking the breath out of me. As I try to force air back into my lungs, I stare down at the man I have caught.

Eyes that seem iridescent stare up at me. I can't tell if they are green, brown or blue, but they are hypnotizing. A lock of red hair falls over a face that is all cheekbones and perfect skin. Soft looking lips are slightly parted. His body is a warm slender weight in my arms. It feels like he belongs in them.

He is a wolf shifter, some distant part of my mind fills in. An omega.

His clothes are red silk. Billowing trousers and a tiny crop top that leaves his perfect midriff bare. It's like some Disney version of what a genie would wear. Or a harem boy, I realize with a shock.

Do I really have one of the harem boys in my arms?

My mind frantically calculates the distance to the front doors and then my car, and compares it to how far away the goons chasing him are. There is a chance we could make it. If I start running right now. And if they don't shoot at us.

I stare into his eyes. I could save him. My feet start to move. I want to save him. But that would mean abandoning the others. Failing my mission before it has even started. It would mean pissing off the Grand Master of the Council.

I swallow over my dry throat, stop my feet from moving and tighten my grip on the boy. Even though he hasn't made the slightest move to try to escape me.

A few heartbeats later the goons arrive. Sweaty and red faced. The boy in my arms looks only slightly disappointed. I set him on his feet, while keeping my hands on him.

"I have him," I say to the goons.

"Who the fuck are you?" asks what appears to be the lead one.

I give him my best malicious grin. "I'm Brodie, the new healer for the harem."

The goons eyebrows disappear into his greasy hairline. "You don't look like a healer."

"Sorry," I say dryly.

"You look ex-military."

It's my turn to raise an eyebrow. "I can't be both?"

The goon huffs and looks at me suspiciously. No doubt I make him uncomfortable because he finds me intimidating. Not a lot I can do about that and it's not like I'm not used to it.

"Hand him over!" he barks.

My heart thuds. "Of course," I say with a smile.

I give the boy a little shove towards the goons. The lead one takes his arm, firmly but not roughly, and I let out a secret sigh of relief.

The boy hasn't taken his beautiful eyes off of me. He doesn't look angry. Or scared. He looks... fascinated? That's the closest I can get to interpreting his stare anyway, and it's going to have to do. It's not like I can ask him.

My gaze sweeps over him again, and my insides do strange things. He is flipping gorgeous. At a truly insane level. But he is the plaything of a billionaire, it's hardly surprising. Like the marble lobby, it's only the very best of the best for Mr. Smithson.

"We'll take the lift back up," says lead goon.

Can't say I really blame him. Thirty floors of stairs isn't my first choice either.

We march out into the lobby and head towards the lifts. It can't look good. Five well muscled men, four in the obligatory black suit uniform of all goons everywhere, all escorting a very pretty boy dressed in garish harem clothes. While one keeps a very firm grip on him.

But there is no one in the lobby to see. And the whole thing probably screams 'crazy rich people shit' and most people have the sense to leave that well alone.

We all crowd into a glass lift, and I can fucking *smell* him. He smells incredible. Jasmine, maybe? I guess it makes sense for a billionaire's sex toy to have great perfume. It probably costs more than my life savings.

He is still staring at me. It's starting to unnerve me. Mostly because I've never been so attracted to anyone. Ever. I feel like a teenager. A very horny teenager who has run into their idol and is sharing a lift with them.

But I'm not a teenager. I'm a grown man. And he is just ridiculously good-looking. Everyone probably swoons in his presence. Even lesbians and straight men. His super power is confusing people about their sexuality. But he can't confuse me, I'm pansexual. People of any, all and no genders can turn my head, which probably makes me even more susceptible to his powers.

Okay, I need to stop spiraling and get a grip. I've met hot people before, there is no need to fall apart. I've got a job to do and I need my wits about me.

The lift opens with a soft ping into a small marble reception area with a huge wooden desk. The goons march over to the giant double doors that are on the far side.

"You need to scan your security pass," barks one of them.

I fish the white plastic card that I was given last night, out of my pocket and hold it up to the reader. The light turns green and the doors swing open to reveal more white marble. This time a long hallway dotted with tall potted plants.

A young man is standing just inside. He is wearing jeans and is bare chested. His pale skin is covered in tattoos. And he has a smattering of piercings.

"Red, Red, Red," he says as he shakes his head.

The boy is shoved forward into his arms.

"What are we going to do with you?" asks the tattooed man in a tone that makes my skin crawl. He isn't angry that the boy tried to escape. He is pleased. Pleased because now he gets to punish him.

"This is the new healer," says the lead goon.

The tattooed man looks up at me and grins. "Nice! I'm Ian, the overseer."

He sticks his hand out, and I shake it while grinning broadly. "I'm Brodie," I say while I fantasize about breaking his neck.

"Come in, come in," says Ian, gesturing at me to step forward.

I do so but I'm surprised to see the goons stay where they are.

"They aren't allowed in the inner sanctum," explains Ian. "Bye boys!" he says as he presses the button to shut the door.

I watch their scowling faces as the door shuts on them, and it's strangely satisfying.

"I'll just lock this one up and then I will give you the grand tour," says Ian.

I nod and watch as he leads the boy away. Red? Is that really his name? Whatever he is called he doesn't struggle. Doesn't fight. He merely walks away docilely. He hasn't so much as murmured since he fell into my arms. Sensible man. Seems he knows there is a time and a place, and sometimes it's just best to surrender. Bide your time and wait for your next opportunity.

Doesn't mean that he is not going to hate me. I caught him. Handed him back to his captors. Brought him back to sexual slavery. My guts churn. He never would have made it anyway. And it was for the greater good. So much work has gone into getting someone in here. I couldn't blow it. Couldn't have Mr. Smithson tighten things up even more.

But Red doesn't know any of that. He can't ever know. My hand flies to my chest as it feels as if my heart literally skips a beat.

Something that feels an awful lot like devastation settles over me like a dark cloud. I'm being absurd. I'm here to do an important job. Not to get insanely good-looking boys to like me. It doesn't matter if he hates me. It doesn't matter at all.

Ian strolls back down the hallway to me. A cocky, nonchalant edge to his stride that sets my teeth on edge. What has he done to Red? What is he going to do to him?

"That was quite an introduction!" he says. "They don't usually escape."

"Good to know," I say with a smile.

He claps me on the back, "Impressed you still managed to be bang on time!"

I shrug, "What can I say, I'm very punctual."

Ian laughs and starts leading the way. The hallway opens up to a huge open space with a full sized stone fountain in it. It's like something you would see on the streets of Paris or in Trafalgar Square. I blink at the monstrosity.

"The boys' rooms are all here."

I look around at the seven doors arranged in a circle around the fountain. Each one is a different color. One is red, the next one blue. The others are pink, green, yellow, purple and gray.

Four hallways, including the one we emerged from, lead off from the circle area around the fountain. One each in the north, east, south and west.

"Up here is the party area."

Ian leads me up a hallway that is to the left of the fountain. We emerge in another cavernous space. It's all sunken seating areas, giant cushions and dark red velvet. It looks like a fourteen-year-old boy's idea of what a brothel looks like.

There is a stage at the far end with a pole on it. In a shadowy corner on the right there is a bar, garishly lit with strips of LED lights. Money clearly cannot buy you taste.

Ian points back towards the fountain. "If you keep going straight across that way, you get to the roof terrace. We have two pools. A fresh water one and a salt water one, because Blue is a siren and Lello is a kelpie."

I nod. "They are all named colors?"

"Yep, but we call Yellow, Lello because he acts like a toddler."

Ian starts leading me back towards the fountain.

"You can fuck them as much as you like. Boss encourages it. It reminds them what they are for and how much they love getting dicked."

It's hard not to falter in my step but I manage it. "Talk about perks of the job!" I grin.

"I know right!" beams Ian as he gives me another slap on the back.

He leads me past the fountain and down another hallway. He opens a sturdy looking door to reveal a brightly lit medical room. I step inside. The examination table dominates the middle of the room. It's a top of the range model, complete with foot stirrups for holding patients' legs up and spread. I swallow. I'm going to be working as a healer for a group of sex slaves. Of course a table with stirrups is going to be needed. I'm going to need good access to the one body part that is going to need the most attention.

I quickly busy myself by rummaging in the drawers and cabinets that line the room. Thankfully, they are painted a pale, inoffensive blue. This room at least, just looks like a well-equipped medical room. I guess Mr. Smithson wasn't interested in designing it. Thank the gods.

"Everything looks great," I say.

It really does. I don't think I've ever had so much equipment and medication at hand. Everything I could possibly need is here.

"There is a touchscreen unit on the wall here, you can place an order for anything you need or to replenish stock," says Ian.

I nod my understanding. Part of me is thrilled to be working in such conditions and the rest of me is disgusted at myself for even contemplating any positives.

Ian opens a plain white door at the right side of the room. "And your bedroom is in here, your stuff has already been delivered."

Over Ian's shoulder I can see an enormous bedroom. With a huge bed, cream-colored shag pile carpet and burgundy velvet curtains.

"Looks great," I manage to say.

"Do you want to settle in?"

"Nah," I shake my head. "I'm good to crack on and make a start. I'd like to examine each of the boys, please."

Ian nods. "No problem, I'll send them in one by one."

I really want him to send Red in first. I want to check he is okay. The need to know that he hasn't been punished awfully is burning through me. Itching along my skin along with the guilt of returning him to this.

But I don't say any of that. I don't show it. I'm a professional and damn good at hiding my emotions. People only see what I want them to see.

"Great!" I smile until my face hurts and Ian finally leaves.

As the door shuts behind him I sigh and run my hands through my hair. It's going to be a long day, and an even longer mission.

Chapter Two

Brodie

The first boy through my door, skips in and hops up onto the examination table. He is dressed in the same Disneyesque version of harem clothes as Red was, but this boy's silk clothes are a daffodil yellow.

His hair is a beautiful golden tumble to his shoulders. He looks up at me with dazzling baby-blue eyes and gives me a beaming smile. My breath hitches. Calling him stunning is like calling the surface of the sun a little warm or a tornado a little breezy.

"Do I get a lollipop?" he asks gleefully.

I did see a jar of lollipops in one of the cupboards. Numbly I fetch one. Hopefully, any minute now my brain is going to come back online.

I hand him the red lollipop and he squeals with delight, does a little wriggle and pops it into his mouth. He sits there sucking it and swinging his legs back and forth.

"You're Lello?" I ask, even though I really don't need to.

He beams at me and nods happily.

"I've never met a kelpie before," I say.

He pops the lollipop out of his mouth. "Everyone says that. The herds do like to stay by the lochs." He has a slight Scottish lilt to his accent and it's adorable.

"But not you?" I ask.

Lello shrugs. "Probably would of, if Daddy didn't find me."

My eyebrows rise. "Daddy is Mr. Smithson?"

He nods.

"He came to Scotland?"

Lello nods happily again and takes his lollipop out of his mouth. "There was this pub by my herd's loch and I liked sneaking off to it to listen to the human music. One night Daddy was there and he caught me."

"Caught you?"

"With a net," says Lello and he sticks the lollipop back in his mouth.

I take a deep breath. "Then what happened?"

Bright blue eyes meet mine. He doesn't look sad or scared. He looks happy. Sweet. Innocent. It doesn't make any sense. I'm so confused right now.

"Daddy took me to his castle, and then he *took* me." He ends with a giggle.

"Were you scared?"

A solemn look flashes across Lello's face. "Yes," he says with a nod. "Very."

Okay, now I am really confused. Is the kelpie not right in his head? Is he being drugged?

"But Daddy claimed me and made me his, and brought me here, in a helicopter!"

Oh crap. I think I know what is going on. I step up to Lello and gently place my hands on his jaw while I stare into his eyes. Carefully I examine under his jaw and down his neck. His mating gland is slightly swollen but I can't feel any teeth marks.

"Did he bite you?"

Lello grins at me, "Yes! He claimed me!" His eyes go all starry looking. As if he is recounting getting an autograph from his favorite pop star.

That fucking bastard Smithson, has made this poor boy imprint on him. Lello thinks he is in love. Kelpie's mate for life. I have no idea if this can be undone.

"But Daddy uses the other boys?" I ask, even though I'm sure he does. But I need to try to get to the bottom of this.

Blue eyes cloud over with pain. "He is human, it's their way."

"Do you only have him?" I ask and the flash of misery and sorrow I see on Lello's face feels like a punch in the gut. He drops his gaze and stares at the floor.

"Need to earn my keep. Not fair to treat me differently," he mumbles.

I'm such a jerk. I really didn't need to bring that up and now I've made this bright, sunshine boy miserable. I know that Smithson doesn't keep his harem exclusive to himself. He uses the boys to entertain people he wants to impress or reward. I didn't need to ask, it was stupid to think that Smithson would have the decency to not make a bonded kelpie sleep with other people.

"Do you want another lollipop?"

And just like that, Lello's exuberant grin is back. I give him a green one this time and he sucks on it happily while I give him a quick exam. Pulse, heart rate. Lung sounds. It is all good.

"Do you need to check down there?" he asks calmly. As if it is no big deal.

"Are you sore?"

He shakes his head and continues sucking away on his new lollipop.

"No need then," I say and he nods distractedly. He seems very engrossed in enjoying the lollipop.

"How often do you get to shift?"

"Whenever I like," he shrugs. "The roof terrace is large, and the pool is great."

"That's good," I answer. "Well, you are good to go, unless you have any aches or pains?"

He shakes his hand and hops down from the table. "Nice to meet you doc!" he calls as he bounces happily away.

I sigh wearily into the sudden silence in my examination room. Neither Lello nor Red are what I was expecting. I'd been imagining trembling terrified boys. It's sure as hell what I would be if I was kept as a sex slave.

My thoughts turn once again to Red. Where is he? What are they doing to him? Is there anything I can do about it, apart from patching him up afterwards?

I wipe down the examination table as I try to gather my thoughts. The door opens again and I turn to face my next patient. His billowing trousers and shimmering crop top is a deep purple. He has short brown hair and hazel eyes. A face that is sheer perfection. I have to blink to make sure I'm not seeing things.

Paranormals do tend to be extremely good looking. Add in Smithson being a creepy powerful billionaire who has no doubt hunted every corner of the earth for the seven boys for his collection, it wouldn't be surprising if this penthouse held the seven most beautiful men on the planet.

I really need to get used to it and stop being stunned by them.

"Purple?" I guess.

He snorts in disgust. "Indigo, but call me that and I'll slap you. My name is Ned."

"Nice to meet you Ned."

He frowns and crosses his arms. "You look too young to be a healer, you what, twenty-five?"

I stare at him for a good few moments. "I'm thirty-four." Nobody has ever thought I look young for my age. What is he playing at?

"Your generation just looks like babies!" he huffs and he barges past me to sit on the examination table.

He is short and slender. His skin has a faint dusky tone to it and I can't see a wrinkle anywhere. He doesn't look a day over twenty-five himself.

"How old are you?" I ask.

"Ninety-eight!" he snaps.

I'm so confused. I glance at the sunlight streaming through the window and then back at Ned.

"Vampire?"

He tilts his head towards the window. "Special glass. UV filter or something."

I don't know what to say to that. It seems very considerate, and that doesn't fit the picture I have built in my head of Smithson. It has to be for his own convenience. He doesn't want to have to wait for nightfall to see all of his collection. It's the only plausible explanation.

"Are you fed enough?" I ask.

"Yes, they bring me people."

That sends a shiver down my spine. I knew I was going to see awful stuff here. Just not that kind. Guess I'll have to emotionally prepare myself for that too. Great.

"Any health concerns?"

"Aside from getting fucked regularly?" he snaps snidely.

I hide my wince. "Can't imagine you are sore from that, vamp healing and all."

He scowls at me. "Suppose you are going to try us all out?"

"You are not my type," I say calmly. He needs to think I'm an asshole, but not so much of an asshole that he makes my life difficult.

Ned raises an eyebrow. "You never would have been hired if you weren't a pervert."

"Never said I wasn't," I reply with a shrug. "I merely said you weren't my type. I like my boys to be pleasant company. Like Red or Lello."

The vampire flows off of the table with a grace that is terrifying to my human senses. He stands toe to toe with me, even though he has to tilt his head up to glare at me.

"Keep your filthy hands off of Lello."

I give him my best sardonic grin. "But I have your permission to fuck Red."

Ned's gaze sweeps over me as if he is looking at something utterly repulsive. "Red can handle you. As can I. I'll keep my mouth shut, if that's what you like."

Hiding my surprise is harder than it should be. The grumpy vampire is really willing to offer himself in Lello's stead? That's very sweet. It indicates that the boys have a close bond. All very useful information.

"Never fucked an old man before," I drawl.

Ned huffs. He isn't the least bit intimidated by me. I like him. If I didn't have to play a douchebag, I think we'd be friends.

"Are we done?" he snaps.

"For now," I mock.

With one last glare, he turns on his heels and seems to vanish. My logical side knows he just walked out at vamp speed but it is still unnerving as hell. How do they stop him from eating everyone and escaping? It shouldn't be possible for humans to keep a vamp who doesn't want to be kept. Even a really young vampire like Ned.

I have so much to uncover. It feels like it is going to take forever.

In the meantime, where the fuck is Red? It feels like it has been hours. I haven't heard any screams or sobbing, but it wouldn't surprise me if this place had sound proofing. And the idea of that is strangely horrifying. They could be torturing him right now and I wouldn't have a clue.

I force myself to take a deep breath. Whatever way they punished him, surely they have finished by now? So why haven't they brought him to me to be fixed up?

And how the hell am I going to ask, without raising suspicion?

This is an absolute nightmare. I already feel as if I am living in hell.

What a great first day.

Chapter Three

Brodie

N o one else has come to the medical room, and it's been fifteen minutes since Ned left. I suspect he was supposed to send someone else in and hasn't, just to be an ass. I definitely like him.

And he has actually helped me. I can use this as an excuse to go find the overseer and while I'm talking to him, I can casually ask about Red. Pretend I'm interested in how he is being punished. Call him a little bitch or something. It's the best course of action I can think of.

The door opens and I whirl to face it. It's Red. He is pushing the door open with his shoulder and his cheeks are flushed. My gaze runs all over his body. He looks fine. I can't see any injuries. He steps in and the door swings shut behind him. Oh shit, his hands are bound behind his back.

"Are you okay?" I ask. There is definitely something off about him.

He holds my gaze steadily, intently. "Not really."

Because of me. It's far harder to hide my wince than it should be. Something flashes across his face and for a stupid moment I think he has read me. But that's impossible. Nobody can read me. I don't give anything away that I don't want to. And this mission is too important, too dangerous. None of the boys can think I'm anything other than a slimeball. What they don't know, can't hurt them.

"That escape attempt was stupid," I say.

He nods and gives me a wry smile. "I know. But someone left the door open after a delivery and it seemed worth a shot."

A spur of the moment, seizing an opportunity, gamble? Sometimes they are worth a shot. Sometimes the luck of being in the right time and the right place is the only thing that works. He was brave to take the chance. But what are the consequences?

"What did they do to you?" I ask gruffly.

Red's eyes narrow a little. "Put a vibrating butt plug in me."

That's what that faint humming noise is? I swallow. My brain reassesses his flushed cheeks, his slightly too fast breathing. His dilated pupils.

Slowly, ever so slowly I let my gaze travel down to his crotch. That's definitely an erection under the red silk. How on earth did I miss all this on my first quick look-over of him?

Because I didn't want to see it. And because I was looking for injuries. Now the room is too hot. My clothes too tight and his forced arousal is consuming all my senses.

"How long do you have to wear it for?" I rasp.

"Until midnight," he says and I watch in fascination as his eyes unfocus for a moment as a shudder racks his body.

It's still morning. That's an awfully long time to be tormented. It looks like the plug has been set at a level to edge him.

For several hours. He is an omega, his body can sustain intense arousal for that long. Damn that's cruel.

I lick my lips. "Why are you here?"

"You can help me."

Silence, thicker than treacle, slides around us. Tying us together with its snaking tendrils. The only sound is the faint hum. I can't hear anything from the outside world. Nothing exists but this room. Nothing but Red, standing before me, aroused and desperate.

My cock doesn't understand the situation and is getting very excited.

"I can't take it out," I say with a calm I do not feel.

He hasn't stopped staring at me since he walked in. It is as if I am the sole focus of his attention and nothing else exists for him.

"You can…" he says quietly, his eyes finally leaving mine but only for the briefest of moments, to flick down to his cock.

I should ask him why the hell he thinks I would do that. That's what a jerk would say. I open my mouth and, "Won't that make it worse?" comes out instead.

He shakes his head very slightly. "It's spelled to edge. Once it senses an orgasm, it will go quiet for a while before starting up again."

So it will give him a break. A reprieve. Some release. And no one will know I had anything to do with it. No one but Red.

"You can't tell anyone I interfered with your punishment," I hear myself say. Apparently I have already decided.

He nods and relief flows across his face chased by a soft whimper that causes him to drop my gaze and bite his bottom lip.

My cock is very, very full. It's because he is an omega. It has to be. He is not in heat, but his arousal is still capable of chucking out some pretty potent pheromones. That is all that's going on. That and he is divinely gorgeous and I have a pulse. A pulse and a sex drive. Of course I'm going to feel discombobulated.

As if in a daze I walk over to the counter and pull on a pair of examination gloves. If I'm wearing gloves, then this is nothing more than a medical procedure. I squirt some lube onto my right hand and grab a wad of tissues with my left.

I return to stand in front of him. He doesn't look awkward or embarrassed. I guess if you have been kept as a sex slave you get a new calibration for what you find humiliating.

He continues to hold my gaze steadily as I lower the waistband on his trousers just enough to free his cock. I wish there was a lock on the door, but it can't be helped. I'm just going to have to be quick.

His cock is as lovely as the rest of him. Larger than I was expecting for an omega and very engorged. It looks uncomfortable. I wrapped my lubed right hand around it. He closes his eyes, tilts his head right back and gives a little sigh that I swear nearly causes me to spill.

Gently, but firmly, I stroke his cock. It throbs in my hand. Hot through the thin silicone membrane of my glove. Is this really happening? I only met him a couple of hours ago. And I am giving him medical assistance, I remind myself sternly. There is nothing romantic about this. It isn't some hot hook up in the toilets of a gay bar either. He probably hates me and is only here out of desperation after trying to rub one out by grinding against his mattress.

That image nearly makes me groan. What the fuck is wrong with me? The thought of some poor captive with his hands bound behind his back and a butt plug up his ass, desperately trying to get some relief, turns me on?

Red moans softly and his body goes taunt. I place the wad of tissues onto the tip of his cock and he spills into them. Nearly silently. After his peak passes, he keeps his eyes closed and tries to calm his breathing, which is only a little fast.

I tuck him back in and then turn away to dispose of the tissues and my gloves. When I turn back to him, he is looking perfectly composed and is back to staring at me intently.

"Thank you," he says solemnly.

I nod. There is no way I can form words when my mouth is this dry. Belatedly I realize he can't open the door from this side because it swings inward and his hands are bound behind his back.

I scramble forward and hold the door open for him. He walks out almost regally and suddenly I'm alone again. This time with the stiffest boner of my entire life. And feeling completely overwhelmed.

What the fuck just happened?

Chapter Four

Brodie

"Sorry about that!" says Ian as he strolls into the examination room without knocking.

"About what?" I ask with my heart hammering. Does he know Red was here? Does he know what happened? Can I make something up that doesn't make me sound soft hearted?

"About keeping you waiting."

"Oh," I huff in relief. "No problem."

Ian grins at me like we are besties and it makes my skin crawl. "Can you come see the next two? It's easier that way."

"Sure," I say as I grab a kit bag and gesture for him to lead the way.

He leads me to the roof terrace and the larger of the two pools. It is a good size but no compensation for the ocean. The noise of the city rumbles far below, and this high up there is a brisk breeze that ripples the surface of the water. I can't see anyone.

Ian puts his fingers in his mouth and whistles loudly. A head emerges, well half a head. I can just make out his eyes. His short jagged hair is blond.

"Come here, Blue!"

The boy swims silently up to us, causing no disturbance in the water. As he gets closer, I can see his eyes are as blue as the Pacific. They are also full of fear and sheer dread.

"This is the new doc, hop out so he can examine you," orders Ian.

Blue obeys, pulling himself out of the pool with a preternatural grace. Water streams off of his naked body and my mind turns to jelly. This is getting too much. They should have found a straight man or a lesbian for this job. It's going to be the death of me.

Blue has a snug fitting black mask over the lower half of his face. Stopping him from singing. The sight ignites a rage deep within me. But long practice keeps it hidden, deep inside me where I know it is going to fester.

"Do you have injuries?" I ask, making sure my tone implies that I don't give a shit.

He holds out his wrist to me. Dark purple bruises encircle it. I gently examine it and I can almost see the hand holding him down. My heart thumps loudly in my ears.

"When did this happen?" I ask.

Blue holds up two fingers.

"Two days ago?"

He nods.

It should have healed far more than this. Sirens are a race with enhanced healing. Something is wrong.

"Is the pool salty enough?" I ask.

His eyes widen in surprise, and he nods.

"How often do you get to sing?"

His gaze flicks to Ian and then back to me. He starts to tremble ever so slightly and he shakes his head.

Never? They never let him sing? How do they not have the faintest clue on how to look after a siren? These people are idiots.

"We need to get a soundproof room built and let him sing regularly, or he is going to get really sick," I say to Ian.

The overseer's eyes widen. "Shit! Okay, no problem man, I'll get people on it."

His reaction mollifies me a little. They were being dim, not purposefully cruel. And it doesn't seem like there is going to be any resistance and delay in carrying out my recommendation. I guess spending money really isn't an issue for Smithson.

"Any other problems?" I ask Blue.

He shakes his head.

"Okay then," I say with a smile.

Suddenly he drops to his hands and knees, presenting his pert, naked ass to me. Offering himself because he thinks that is what he needs to do for me, because it usually is what he needs to do.

Ian chuckles gleefully. The man is such a bastard. I walk around to Blue's head and drop down into a squat. My fingers find his chin and tilt his face to look up at me. His eyes are wide and frantic. This is what I was expecting all the boys to be like.

"Thank you for your kind offer, Blue. But I'm working right now. You can get back in the pool."

A soft splash and he is gone. These boys can move fast. I get back to my feet.

"Great work ethic, doc," says Ian. "Guess you can come back later and fuck him. Though personally I find all his whining and tears grating."

I grind my teeth. "Who would you recommend?"

He barks a laugh, "All of them! Apart from Blue and Gray."

"Why not Gray?"

"You'll see, that's who we are visiting next."

"Lead the way."

I follow behind the overseer and think of all the inventive ways he could die. Hopefully, by my hands. Maybe this little fantasy is the thing that is going to keep me sane.

Ian takes me back to the obscene fountain. He turns to the gray door. There is a keypad by it that I didn't notice before. My observation skills really are slipping.

"The code is 666," he laughs, as if it's the best joke ever.

We step inside the dimly lit room and every hair on my body stands on end as my primal senses scream at me to flee. It takes all my effort to ignore ten thousand years of evolution and its self-preservation honed instincts. But somehow I do.

There is nothing but a huge bed in the windowless room. A pentagram and other symbols I do not recognize are carved into the ceiling and painted in red. I can just make out tips of another devil's trap peeking out from under the bed, where I'm assuming a mirror image is etched into the floor.

The bed is draped with gray silk sheets. A boy is lying on his back, spread eagle. Wrists and ankles chained with heavy manacles to each corner of the bed. The same ridiculous harem outfit covers his body. A body that is sheer youthful male perfection.

The gray silks look good on him, but then again, anything would look good on him.

The lower half of his face is covered by a similar black mask to Blue's, though I seriously doubt this one is to stop singing.

Tousled dark hair falls over his eyes. Eyes that are glowing a baleful red and glaring at me.

With some great difficulty, I swallow. "Smithson is insane,"

Ian laughs and I realize with horror that I have said those words out loud.

"I know right? Demons live for millennia and fucking invented words like grudge and revenge. Gray will get free at some point." Ian shudders and I can tell he is actually scared. Not a dumb man after all.

"So, I guess we are super nice to Gray?" I say.

Ian laughs and slaps me on the back. "Damn right we are!"

Gingerly, I step towards the bed. I should examine him. But what for? I don't think even decapitation can kill a demon. And I'm really not sure I'm brave enough to touch him.

I inch a little closer and Gray lifts his head up off the pillow and growls. A low deep sound that echoes off the walls and claws into my soul. It's not a sound of this realm, it's not anything human ears should ever hear. It's absolutely not something that the pretty-looking boy lying in front of me should be able to make.

My body overrules me, and steps hastily back. Fuck this.

"He looks fine," I announce.

Ian laughs again. "Don't blame you man, you look whiter than a ghost!"

He is still laughing as we walk out. As soon as the door shuts behind us, I feel guilty.

"He is fed, washed and all that?" I ask.

"Yeah, yeah. Of course," dismisses Ian as he waves his hand about. "Gotta look after the boss's expensive property."

His words grate on me. I could really do with a lie down about now. There is an awful lot to process, and it's not surprising that I have a headache coming on.

"Jade and Pink are on the island with the boss, they will be back tomorrow, so I guess you get to chill for the rest of the day, dude."

"The boys leave the penthouse?" I'm pretty sure my question just sounds like idle curiosity.

"The well behaved ones do."

"So not Gray then?" I say in my best sardonic tone.

Ian laughs as if I am the most hilarious person he has ever met. He claps me on the back yet again and I can feel my eyes bulging with barely contained fury. I do not want this man touching me. Ever.

"I like you, bro. You are gonna fit right in here."

With that, he shoves his hands in his jean pockets and strolls away whistling. I watch him go for a moment and indulge in a few more fantasies. Then I head for my room. Time to unpack, get settled and have that much needed lie down. I have a feeling that tomorrow is going to be every bit as crazy as today.

Nothing more than I deserve. As the saying goes, no rest for the wicked.

Chapter Five

Red

I always feel calm when I am putting my makeup on. I don't know what it is about the process that is so soothing, but I'm just glad to have something to fall back on. A crutch, a sticky plaster, a tool. Whatever helps me get through the day.

I'm trying to tell myself that I'm taking extra care and getting extra glammed up because Ritchie is coming today and I want to stay in his good books. Keep him happy with me. Especially after my lousy escape attempt. Appeasing the boss is always a good idea, but I have a sneaky suspicion that I also want to look good for the new healer, Brodie.

He is a very good-looking man. All tall and brooding with muscles. And perhaps I have finally completely lost my mind, but I swear I see kindness and compassion in his hazel eyes.

He caught me and ended my bid for freedom, but I'm pretty certain he didn't want to. And he has been decent so far. He has checked all the boys that are here and been kind and professional while doing so. He has taken no one to his bed, and he has been here twenty-four hours.

And he helped me. I watch my reflection in the mirror as a flush spreads across my cheeks. My makeup brush pauses mid air. I need to wait until my blush fades, otherwise the colors will be all wrong.

The feel of his gentle hand had been exquisite. It had been so long since anyone had touched me with kindness.

My heart thuds. I'm being an idiot. A tiny dollop of decency and I'm swooning like a Victorian maiden. Have I really become that pathetic, that desperate for affection? So much so, that I'm seeing it when it's not even there? Brodie was probably just being professional, nothing more. And him being less of a jerk than the people we normally get, is not a reason to get all starry-eyed.

The lights flash three times. Ritchie's helicopter has landed on the helipad. He will be here in a few minutes. I hastily finish applying my makeup and then dart off to where I'm supposed to be when he enters the penthouse. On the stage with the other boys. Looking pretty.

I'm the last to get there. I give Blue's hand a quick squeeze then everyone stands in front of him. I take my place at the front. If Ritchie has brought guests, I want their eyes on me. It's the least I can do, to help save the others.

Lello stands beside me, hopping from foot to foot and nearly vibrating with excitement.

Voices and footsteps sound in the hallway. I stand up taller. Ritchie turns the corner surrounded by a good sized entourage. My heart sinks. He has brought guests. Quite a few of them. Just wonderful.

My gaze sweeps over Jade and Pink. They look physically unharmed. I have no idea how they are doing mentally. Both of them have excellent poker faces. I'm going to have to wait till later to find out.

Lello lets out a shriek of joy and bounds forward. He jumps up into Ritchie's arms, wrapping his legs around the human's waist. Ritchie grins and puts his hands on Lello's ass.

"Did you miss me baby?" he asks.

"Yes, Daddy!" exclaims Lello exuberantly.

Poor fucking kid. Of all the awful things Ritchie has done, I think this is the one I hate him the most for. I'm so fucking glad he has never tried to mate me. I can only guess that he did his research and discovered wolf shifter omegas don't become infatuated with a bite.

"Gonna be my good boy?" says Ritchie.

Lello nods and bounces up and down in Ritchie's arms like an overexcited puppy. I watch as Ritchie carries Lello to his room, and I want to be sick.

But there are guests to make comfortable and serve drinks to. And I need to try to keep them from noticing Blue. The rest of us can cope with servicing a customer far better than he can. Nevermind that his obvious terror attracts the very worst of bastards.

Plastering on my best smile, I slink into the small crowd to introduce myself.

A little while later, Ritchie strolls back into the party room looking like the cat that got the cream. I want to punch him so hard. Everything about him repulses me. From his backwards baseball cap, his tech bro clothes and his silicon valley golden boy attitude. He is in his forties now but clearly still thinks it's the turn of the millennium and he is a twenty something genius. When in reality he had one good idea at the right time and the right place and has been riding that wave ever since.

I can't believe I ever liked him. The memory of that is so humiliating. I can only hope that I was blinded by his wealth and not missing all my brain cells.

My gaze flicks over to Lello's door. Can I slip away? I cast a furtive glance around. No one is looking at me. Blue is tucked safely in a corner. It looks like I'm good to go.

I drift towards Lello's door, just in time to see Brodie slipping in. My heart does a little skip. The last healer never checked on us. He'd only see people if we carried them to the med room.

I ease myself through the half-open door. Lello is sprawled naked on his front. His fingers still clutching the garish yellow sheets. He is out cold, and Brodie is checking his pulse.

"Is he okay?" I ask.

Brodie nods. "Fainted. Probably from the intensity of being bitten."

My gaze flicks to the fresh teeth marks on Lello's neck and I shudder. I walk over to Lello's bathroom and run a washcloth under the hot tap. I bring it back to the bed and gently clean Lello up. As I finish, he stirs.

I hand Brodie the dirty cloth and he takes it without quibble.

"Daddy?" cries Lello.

I sit on the bed next to him. "He has gone back to the party, sweetie."

Lello sobs. A lost, lonely, heartbroken sound that I feel in my gut.

"Do you want a cuddle?" I ask. I'm a poor substitute for who his instincts think is his mate, but it's the only thing I can offer.

Lello nods and crawls onto my lap. I hold him like a baby and smooth his hair while he cries. His body is thrumming with distress. In the natural order of things, after reaffirming the mating bond, his mate would be here. Soothing him, holding him, cherishing him.

The absence must be bewildering and terrifying for Lello's subconscious.

My gaze meets Brodie. He is standing silently by the foot of the bed. He holds my gaze steadily and I am not imagining the sorrow and the rage that I am seeing in his eyes.

He nods at me and slips quietly away. I don't think Lello even noticed he was there. Now he has gone to give the little kelpie some privacy. I was right. Brodie is a good man.

So what the hell is he doing here?

Chapter Six

Brodie

I guess I'm not supposed to be here, but hopefully by lurking unobtrusively in the background, no one will notice me to send me away. A party doesn't require a healer. Not that I would class it as a party. Smithson and his friends are just sprawled around on the overstuffed sofas while the boys serve them drinks. Quiet jazz music is barely audible. I think these men love the sound of their own voices over anything else.

A boy in bright pink is sitting on someone's lap. He has to be Pink, one of my patients that I haven't met yet. He looks very young and very human, which is interesting. I thought the harem were all paranormals. He is of course, jaw droppingly good looking. Forty-eight hours ago I would have said he was the most beautiful boy I had ever seen. But now I have seen Red and I don't think anyone else will ever compare.

I can't see Jade from where I'm standing but I think he is sitting on the floor by someone's feet. A movement on the other side of the room catches my attention. I turn my head slightly, just in time to see Ned gracefully dropping to his knees in front of the open legs of one of the guests. My eyebrows rise. Putting your dick in the mouth of an angry vampire is a completely deranged thing to do.

That train of thought is stopped by Red slipping quietly out of Lello's room and coming to join me.

"He is asleep," says Red, answering my unasked question.

I nod and tear my gaze away, back to the party. Red without makeup is mesmerizing. Red with gorgeous makeup is making every brain cell I have screech to a halt.

My gaze falls on Ned's bobbing head and I snatch it away to stare blankly at the empty stage. I don't need to see that. And he doesn't need any more of an audience.

"How do they make Indigo behave?" I ask, using Ned's harem name because that is what an asshat would do.

"Ritchie has his great grandkids," Red whispers.

Red referring to Smithson by such a familiar name, really gets my back up for some reason, but I shove the feeling aside to concentrate on what he just told me. Shit. That's awful. Awful for Ned and awful for everything. Not only is he not going to be onboard with any plan, he may well actively inform. I'm going to have to leave him out of everything. It fucking sucks. I like the vampire.

Suddenly Smithson jumps to his feet. "Clive, Brian, Eric! Come meet Gray, you'll love him!"

Three of the men obediently follow behind Smithson. The overseer joins them, grinning broadly. My heart is hammering.

"Gray fights like fuck but once you get it in, he loves it and can't get enough," boasts Smithson to his little gang.

Helplessly, I watch them all file into Gray's room and shut the door. My gaze finds Red's.

"He is an incubus," explains Red, confirming that Smithson isn't talking complete shit.

I blink in surprise. "Surely an incubus would thrive in a harem, enjoy it?" Gray did not seem happy at all when I did my half-assed check on him.

Red shrugs. "He was summoned hundreds of years ago and has been owned by one cruel human after another. I guess it has been too much, even for a demon."

More shit news. If his summoner is dead, it could be nigh on impossible to send him back to Hell. And if he is all fury and wrath, freeing him is not an option. Another complication. Oh well, it wasn't like this was ever going to be easy.

A terrifying growl followed by a snarl reverberates from Gray's room. My heart rate doubles and my breathing quickens. My body wants to run. Far, far away and never look back. Adrenaline is making my muscles shake in preparation.

Those asshats in there are either incredibly brave or incredibly stupid. I know which one my money is on.

A new noise flows out of Gray's room. A scared, hopeless sound. A cry of fear and pleading.

Red's hand is on my shoulder. I've taken a step towards the room. Red holds my gaze steadily and shakes his head. He is right. Bursting in there will achieve nothing. I have to stand here and listen while each desperate wail causes a little piece of my soul to wither and die. This is the stuff of nightmares. This is the stuff I had told myself I had braced myself for. But the reality of it is far, far worse than anything my imagination had dreamed up.

After what feels like an eternity, the noises turn more carnal. It's not a relief. Gray is an incubus, he feeds on sex, it is his sustenance. A primal need for survival is not consent.

A few feet away, the guests that stayed in the party area, are carrying on drinking and groping the boys. As if they can't hear a thing. Or they don't give a shit because they are soulless beings without a shred of compassion within them. I've never wanted to commit mass murder before and I'm not even ashamed of the thought. These fuckers deserve to die. Painfully.

Eventually, Gray's door opens and the assailants file out, all with varying grins and smirks on their faces. I watch as they get settled back on the sofas and then I make a beeline for Gray's room, with Red right beside me.

As I step inside my stomach heaves. His mask has been replaced with a ballgag and tears are tracking down his face. His eyes aren't glowing red, they are a very human, very traumatized looking brown.

Red hurries up to him and removes the ball gag before disappearing into the bathroom. Why did they bother swapping the mask for the gag? Oh fuck, it was because they wanted to hear him, wasn't it? My fists clench so hard, I'm going to pull a tendon.

Red comes back with a wet cloth.

"No, it's better for him if you leave it. Let him absorb the sustenance," I say. Let one tiny bit of good come from this abomination.

Red's eyes widen, and he nods. He takes the cloth and gently cleans Gray's face with it instead. Seemingly fearless of the demon. Now I feel all kinds of shitty for my reaction when I first met Gray. I didn't treat him as a person. Maybe I'm not pretending to be a douchebag. Maybe I really am one.

I watch uselessly as Red finishes cleaning Gray's face. Red then fiddles with a lever on the wall and the chains loosen. I step back warily, but Gray merely shuffles up to a sitting position and takes the glass of water Red gives him with shaking hands. He drinks it down eagerly, so Red refills it. Gray drinks the second glass down too.

"Want some more?" asks Red gently.

Gray shakes his head. The gesture startles me, as if part of me didn't think he was capable of human communication. His eyes keep settling on me warily.

"This is Brodie, the new healer, you don't need to worry about him," says Red.

Gray immediately looks more relaxed. He trusts Red. That is good to know. And all very endearing. Especially the bit about Red deeming me trustworthy.

"I need a piss." Gray's voice is low and husky. Rasping and quiet. But very human sounding. It sends shivers down my spine, not because I'm scared, but because I am finally fully understanding that while he is a demon, he is still a person.

Red kneels down by the bed and pulls out a urine bottle. I grimace, but Gray doesn't seem to care. He merely takes it. I turn away as he fills it. I turn back when I see him out of the corner of my eye, handing the bottle to Red. Red calmly carries it to the bathroom as if it's no big deal.

The bedroom door opens and the overseer walks in with a tray. He looks surprised to see me. Then his gaze flicks to Red who is walking out of the bathroom.

"Get back to the party!" snaps Ian.

Red darts off without so much as a glance in my direction.

"What was he doing here?" asks Ian.

I shrug. "Wanted to play nurse."

Ian huffs and places the tray on Gray's lap. There is a plate on it with a very rare steak. No cutlery though. But judging by the way Gray's eyes have lit up, he doesn't mind. He picks it up with his hands and starts gnawing on it.

"Is he alright?" asks Ian.

"Yeah, he is fine. Good idea to feed him after working him hard," I drawl.

Ian chuckles, "Like we said, good idea to be super nice to the demon."

I force a laugh out of my throat. I'm going to be sick. Hopefully, I can aim it at Ian and spew all over him.

"Red was great at being a nurse, is it okay if I get him to assist me?" I say, instead of vomiting.

"Can't see why not, as long as he is not supposed to be bending over somewhere."

The admonishment is soft. Ian is reasonable to fellow humans.

"My bad!" I exclaim as an apology. As much as it hurts my soul I need Ian to like me.

Ian grins, "No worries, we all have our favorites."

I give the overseer my best lecherous smirk. Fuck, he is so right. Red is my favorite, just not in the way he is thinking. It's shameful that I've made it obvious. But more importantly, how the hell did it happen and what on earth am I going to do about it?

Chapter Seven

Brodie

I'm grouchy and sleep deprived but I need to push past it. I was up all night, haunted by the memory of Gray's cries, but It wouldn't be fair to take my bad mood out on the boys. They really don't deserve it. They need kindness and care, and I just wish I was better at those things. A heavy sigh escapes me. It is probably for the best that I'm not. It's going to make it easier to maintain my cover.

I chuck my clipboard down with a little more force than is necessary. The full inventory of the equipment and supplies in the examination room is done. What now?

The door opens and Pink shuffles in. "Red said you need to examine everyone."

I make a mental note to thank Red. I need to check and meet Pink and I really need something to do. Red sending him here is fantastic.

"That's right," I nod. "Hop up onto the table."

He walks past me and does as I asked. Our eyes met. His are a burnished shade of brown, they should be beautiful, but the dull, lifeless look in them is spine chilling. There is an emptiness to his gaze. The look of someone who has given up.

"You're human?" I ask.

He nods. "A vessel."

Ah, okay, that solves that mystery. He is like me, human but with an innate magic that makes us part of the paranormal community. I know little about vessel's. Except they are usually born to an ethnic group that call themselves Old Blood and most of them are Lords and Ladies. The old ruling class of Britain.

Vessels are humans who naturally absorb magic but cannot wield it. They are usually given to a mage who fucks them to take the magic. And magic enjoys being free so vessel's bodies are driven to seek release, going into something similar to a heat.

I guess that's why Smithson wanted one for his collection. A boy who gets desperately and insanely horny is going to be fun if you are a sick, twisted bastard. Poor Pink.

I've never had a vessel as a patient before. Apart from his magic, Pink is human. With all the weaknesses, slow healing and vulnerabilities that entails. Out of all the seven boys, he is the one who is going to need my care the most.

But how did he get here? Abducting paranormal boys is one thing, it's not like their families can call the police, for risk of the paranormal world being discovered, but a human? And presumably from a wealthy, powerful family.

"Does your family know where you are?" I ask.

"Yes, they sold me to Ritchie," he says tonelessly as if it doesn't matter.

My stomach knots. Fucking hell. Poor kid. Some people really don't deserve to have children. Doing that to your own child? That is beyond evil.

"How old are you?"

"Eighteen."

Just a baby. Nobody that young should have that world-weary look in their eyes. The look of someone who has been through too much. Kicked down so often that they can no longer get up. Fuck Ritchie, fuck Pink's parents. Fuck this cruel world.

I take a deep breath. "Any health concerns?"

"My hole is sore," he says calmly as if discussing the weather.

"Alright, let me take a look."

Pinks scoots his stupid billowing trousers off, lays back and puts his legs on the stirrups. There is no sign of any embarrassment or shyness.

Carefully I examine him. I have to ease a gloved, lubed finger inside him to check for internal lacerations, but he just stares at the ceiling and doesn't flinch. Pink clearly no longer gives a fuck about anything.

"Okay, you can get dressed now."

I dispose of the gloves and wash my hands. When I finish, I turn back to Pink to find him calmly sitting on the examination table. Dressed and completely unruffled.

I hand him a tube of ointment.

"I can't find any tears. Apply this three times a day and try to stretch and lube up well if you know you are going to be working."

He nods as if he has heard this a thousand times before, which I'm sure he has. I want to do more for him. So much more. But this is going to have to do for now.

He hops down off of the table. "Thank you," he says politely and then he is gone.

I'm staring at the closed door but I can't help it. My heart is heavy and my thoughts are tangled. I could quit. I could pack my bags and tell Smithson I've changed my mind. But running away would be cowardly. It would mean abandoning these boys. And the plan assumes Smithson would let me go. He could well decide that I know too much to be allowed to walk away.

I need to man up. If these boys can suffer this torment, then I can observe it.

Numbly I turn and start wiping down the examination table. The movements familiar and soothing. The false comfort of routine, tricking my mind into believing that everything is as it should be.

The door opens again. It seems no one in this place knocks. I guess sex slavery and ideas of privacy are not concepts that go together well.

Judging by the vivid green silks my visitor is wearing, this is Jade. The last remaining boy to meet. His hair is so pale it is nearly white and it has been hacked off short. Leaving spikes sticking up every which way. I wonder if he did it to himself. I can't see his eyes or his face, because he is staring determinedly at the floor.

He sits on the table and waits silently. I can't figure out what type of paranormal he is. He is slender and has pale milky skin but many different beings have those characteristics.

"What kin are you?" I ask.

He looks up at me with moss green eyes. "I'm part fey."

Fey? That can't be right. The fey realm drifted away hundreds of years ago. There haven't been any fey on Earth for generations.

"There is a breeding program. Revivalists search for humans with fey ancestry and breed them, concentrating the bloodline each generation."

I blink at him in shock. I'm grateful for the explanation but that's a lot to take in. And super fucked up. Ethics and morals aside, as a healer it leaves me in a quandary. What's a healthy resting heart rate for someone who is part fey? What is their normal healing speed? I'm going to have to keep a close eye on Jade.

"Any health problems?" I manage to croak out.

He drops his gaze and shakes his head. I run my gaze over him again. Now he has said it, I can really see it. I can easily picture him haughtily reclining on a throne in somewhere called a court of something and other. It's where he should be, instead of here, sitting slumped in my examination room, shame etched into every line of his body, while dressed in absurd Jasmine the Disney princess clothes.

Silently I listen to his heart and his lung sounds, even though I do not know what I am looking for. It's clear he is hating every moment of my touch, so I try to be as brisk as possible while keeping actual contact to a minimum. It's a good thing he doesn't need an internal exam, I'm not sure he could cope with it.

But luckily he doesn't, and everything I have checked seems good, if he was fully human. It's what I'm going to have to go by. I have no other stats to base his vitals on. Human will have to do, and he is part that too.

"May I leave now?" he says softly, still looking at the floor.

I sigh. "Of course, but any problems, you come and see me, okay?"

He nods and flows out of my room with a grace that clearly marks him as paranormal. It's both unnerving and alluring at the same time. Though I can't help thinking that the way Red moves is more enticing.

Shaking my head to clear it before I fall down that rabbit hole of thoughts and daydreams, I consider my situation.

I've met all seven boys now. And I've already discovered some useful information. Now I just need to unearth more. A lot more. So I can burn this place down.

Chapter Eight

Red

Even though my back is to the door, I know when Brodie enters the kitchen. Some part of me senses his presence. I glance over my shoulder to flash him a quick smile. He is standing in the doorway, still and silent. Taking in the sight before him. He is wearing his usual stony expression, but I can tell he is surprised. It's understandable, the kitchen is nice. Light and airy and not garish like the rest of the penthouse.

And with me cooking and the others sitting around the table, I suppose it does rather look like a scene of domestic bliss. Ned and Lello are playing cards. Jade is puzzling over the crossword in the morning paper, while Pink is staring at something on his tablet.

Brodie comes and joins me by the cooker. "Want a hand? I'm brilliant at flipping pancakes."

Well, I can't resist that. With a grin, I relinquish the frying pan and concentrate on the bacon. Brodie hums a tune under his breath and executes a perfect pancake flip. I give him a round of applause and he beams like a kid. My heart stutters for a moment giving me a strange fluttering sensation in my chest. He is so handsome when he smiles. It should be illegal.

I want him to smile at me like that every day. All day. I want it to be the first thing I see in the morning, and the last thing I see at night.

Shit! I'm nearly burning the bacon. What is wrong with me? Why am I having such crazy thoughts about the new healer? He is a decent man, but that is no reason to imprint on him like Lello has on Ritchie. Oh my god, that's not what's happened is it? Wolf shifters don't imprint, but this is an unnatural situation. Maybe it's some kind of twisted sideways Stockholm Syndrome?

"Are you okay?"

His low rumble nearly has me jumping out of my skin but I recover with my best winning smile.

"I'm fine."

Hurriedly, I dish up breakfast. Busying myself with the simple task and avoiding eye contact with Brodie, as if he would be able to read all my secrets if I looked at him. I quickly serve Pink and Jade, and their thanks warms my heart.

"Lello, can you take a plate to Blue? Ned, can you take one to Gray?" I say.

They both get up and come to collect a plate. Seemingly happy with their assigned tasks. But Ned wrinkles his nose in disgust.

"Solid food is disgusting," he comments.

Lello giggles. "You are so silly!"

"I'm not silly!" grumbles Ned as he walks out of the kitchen with Lello.

Brodie is watching them leave. He turns to me. "Are they together?"

My hand flies up to my mouth in an effort to contain my gasp. "Don't let Ned hear you say that! He thinks of Lello as a kid!"

"Oh, sorry!" says Brodie, and he looks a little embarrassed and ashamed.

I shake my head. "It's fine, it is a rather wholesome relationship for a harem."

His hazel eyes fix on mine and now I'm just standing in the kitchen staring at him. He still looks guilty for thinking sordid things about Ned and Lello but there are a whole lot more emotions swirling through him as he stares back at me. I can't begin to name them. But they are intense and they give my stomach butterflies.

"Let's eat!" I say a little too loudly.

He blinks and looks a little dazed, as if he is coming out of a spell. Then he gives me a soft smile, takes a plate of pancakes and bacon, and makes his way to the table.

I follow after him shamelessly fast. And I take the seat right next to him. Because apparently I can't control myself around him at all. This is embarrassing. I'm not a teenager with a crush.

"You have to cook your own food?" asks Brodie casually, but I can hear the disapproval in his voice.

"No, there is a chef on staff and we can order in whenever we like. But I enjoy cooking and it's nice to have something to do." I wince. I'm pretty sure my unspoken, *other than spread my legs*, is as clear as day.

Brodie doesn't comment on it though. He merely nods his understanding and takes a bite of pancake. His eyes close and he lets out a little moan. My cock twitches. What would he sound like in bed? Does he sound like that? I feel my cheeks heat so I quickly look down to examine my own plate before he sees.

Am I going into heat? Is that what is wrong with me? I don't think so. I can't feel any heat symptoms. Apart from horniness. But this horniness is just for Brodie. Fuck. I really do have a crush. This is the last thing I need.

I sigh. Maybe it will be fine. It could be a fun distraction from the hellhole that is my life. A crush would be something else to think about. Occupy my time with. He is allowed to sleep with me, it's not against the rules. In fact, it's positively encouraged. So I could plan all sorts of elaborate ways to seduce him.

Seduce him. Like walk into the med room and demand that he jerks me off. I nearly choke on my pancake as that memory comes flooding back in full vivid detail. Well, he didn't seem to object. And I swear his feelings about it weren't entirely professional. So seducing him shouldn't be too much of a challenge. And then maybe once I've itched that scratch, it will go away.

Now I'm feeling sad. Is it because I want it to be a challenge? Or because I don't want the itch to go away? I have no idea. I've finally cracked and lost my mind. Not surprisingly, given what I have had to endure over the last few years.

But it's fine. I don't need my sanity to seduce Brodie. The pursuit and the prize will both be highly enjoyable. And I'm damn curious to discover why he is here. I suspect it will take a lot more than pillow talk to get Brodie to spill his secrets. But I might glean some clues.

I take a sip of orange juice and hide my grin. I was right. Having something else to do is great. I've only just decided to embark on this plan and I'm already having fun.

For the first time in a long time, I'm looking forward to what the future may bring. It's a damn good feeling.

Chapter Nine

Brodie

I can't get into this book at all, but I have literally nothing else to do. Young paranormals are the least likely of all the people on the planet to need medical attention. And I only have seven to look after. It really doesn't give me much to do. As for my real work, snooping around only ever succeeds in raising suspicions. All my interactions need to be natural and unforced. Which brings me back to having nothing to do.

My employment contract states that I'm not to leave the penthouse for the first six months of my employment. So going out is not an option. Not that I would want to anyway, in case I was needed. In my experience, emergencies never happen when it is convenient.

Lello graciously said I could use his pool, but it's unheated, in an effort to replicate a Scottish loch, and bloody freezing. I'm not a masochist. There is a well-equipped gym, but there are only so many hours of the day I can work out.

I expected this mission to be many things. Boring was not one of them. How do the boys cope? Some of them have been trapped here for years.

Suddenly, the lights flash, startling me from my musings. I stare at the light fixture in confusion for a moment before it belatedly hits me. It's the signal that Smithson's helicopter has landed on the helipad that's on the roof of the penthouse.

I put my book down and jump to my feet. I'm excited and relieved that something is happening, and that makes me an awful person. Smithson is here, and that means only one thing. One or more of the boys are going to be used. And I'm fucking excited about it because I won't be bored anymore. There is something seriously wrong with me. I'm not a nice person at all.

My self-awareness doesn't stop me from making my way to the party area. As a healer I don't need to be here. I probably shouldn't be here at all. But I take up the same shadowy corner that I lurked in last time. Hopefully, it will work again and no one will notice me. If they do, I can just claim that I'm over diligent. Or confess to being bored. Either will work.

I watch as the boys start to assemble on the stage. Blue slinks in, still dripping wet and the others let him stand at the back. The sight warms my heart. I love that the boys have a bond and care for each other. They have clearly accepted that Blue is the most vulnerable and they are all willing to do what they can to protect him.

Red takes up position at the front. I know what he is doing. He is trying to draw attention to himself because he wants to protect them all. Protect them all and sacrifice himself. It's all very noble and it makes me like him even more. Red is kind, nurturing, stupidly brave and ridiculously good looking. I never thought I'd meet anyone like him.

And that's not what I am here to do. This isn't a frigging speed dating event. I need to stop thinking about him like that. It's unprofessional. I'm better than this. At least I used to be. Once upon a time.

Smithson strolls into the party area with just one guest and I breathe a sigh of relief. Just one guest is a lot less for the boys to have to deal with.

The guest looks like a Chinese businessman. I don't think I recognize him from any rich list. It makes me wonder just how many humans are discovering that paranormals exist thanks to Smithson? No wonder the Council is pissed off. Though maybe Smithson just tells his guests his harem is merely human? And any strangeness is just an act? It's definitely something that I need to find out.

Smithson holds his arms out wide. "There they are! Ritchie's Rainbow!"

I'm nearly sick in my mouth but I manage to keep my bile down. He seriously calls them that? It has to be the most cringeworthy thing I have ever witnessed. He probably refers to himself in third person too.

Lello gives a little squeal of delight and bounces off the stage and into Smithson's arms again.

"Always so happy to see me, aren't you baby?" grins Smithson.

"Yes, Daddy!" Lello exclaims happily.

I expect Smithson to carry Lello off again. But this time he carries the kelpie over to the sofa facing the stage and sits down, arranging Lello on his lap.

"Which one do you want to join you?" Smithson asks his guest.

The businessman looks a little sweaty and I can't say I blame him. That's quite a smorgasbord of choice. I don't realize that I'm holding my breath until he points at Pink. I'm such an asshat, it's hardly like Pink deserves it anymore than Red.

The vessel steps calmly off of the stage and goes and sits next to Smithson's guest.

"Red, dance for us!" calls Smithson.

My mouth has gone dry. Red nods and the rest of the boys scurry away from the stage. The lights lower until there is just a soft glow on Red. Music starts to play. I watch mesmerized as Red walks up to the pole. First, he merely places one hand on it and then he *moves.*

My mouth is hanging open but there is not a single thing I can do about it. Red caresses the pole. His beautiful body undulates around it. The stupid harem clothes leave his midriff bare and I can see his muscles flowing as he moves in perfect time to the music. He moves with grace and skill and it is the hottest thing I have ever seen.

The positions he melts into take my breath away. From the long lines of his legs, to the way his back arches, to the way he draws all attention to his pert ass. He shimmies his hips and my cock swells. The only thought I have in my head is the desire to be inside him and to be the cause of him moving like that.

I tear my gaze away before I do something embarrassing like come in my pants. My gaze falls on Pink kneeling between the guest's legs and sucking him off while the man's full attention is on Red. I swallow and snatch my gaze away, this time my attention falls on Smithson. Just in time to see him unceremoniously dump Lello off of his lap and onto the sofa next to him.

Smithson stands and the music stops. He holds out his hand to Red. Red's face is perfectly blank as he solemnly takes Smithson's hand. He gracefully steps off the stage and follows the billionaire to his room.

Lello stares after them. His expression is all dismay, heartbreak, jealousy and rejection. It's like looking at a puppy who is being left behind. The thing is, as ludicrous and unwarranted as it may be, I have a horrible feeling that I have the exact same expression on my face.

I'm so screwed.

Chapter Ten

Red

The hot water of the shower feels good. It is washing Ritchie off of me. As I watch the water swirl down the drain, I wish it could wash away all my regrets too. Take away all my mistakes and restore my youth and my innocence.

But it's only water. It does not have that power. It can only clean and that is going to have to do.

As I look around the vast marble and chrome expanse I am standing in, it's hard to remember there was a time I was awed by it. Impressed and thinking luxury like this was worth anything. How foolish was I. A huge shower head and a tropical rainforest setting is worth nothing.

"Be nice to yourself" I mutter to the empty space.

I had grown up in poverty. I was young. Being dazzled was understandable and does not make me a bad person. Everyone makes mistakes.

"Stop," I say to the shower.

It beeps softly and obeys me. I take a warm, fluffy towel from the heated towel rail but I can't muster up the enthusiasm to dry myself off. So I just sling it around my waist. I open the bathroom door and nearly walk straight into Brodie.

His gaze drops down to my wet naked chest but only lingers for a heartbeat before returning to meet my eyes, this time with his cheeks flushed.

"I... um... wanted to check how you are?" he stammers.

I smile. He clearly wants me, but something about his attention does not feel like other men's. His feels genuine. As if he wants me, and not just my body. It might just be my fantasy, but it is a nice one and I am keeping it.

"He didn't hurt me," I say.

Brodie's warm hazel eyes do not look convinced. "Maybe not physically," he mutters.

"You fix minds too?" I snap and instantly regret it. I didn't want to be catty, it just came out.

Brodie winces. "No, you are right, I'm sorry."

An apology? I'm not used to those. I'm used to men who get offended at the slightest thing and who would never admit to being wrong in a hundred years. And Brodie didn't even do anything wrong, he is just concerned for me, which is sweet. And now I'm just standing here, staring at him and dripping water onto the floor.

Clothes. I should put clothes on. That would be a great idea. For some strange reason, it's hard to tear my gaze away from Brodie's eyes, but I manage it.

I walk over to the large closet and throw open the door. At least I never have to decide what to wear. Several identical red outfits glare back at me. I swear I have forgotten what it feels like to wear jeans. And tops that actually cover my stomach.

"You sleep in the closet?" Brodie's voice sounds horrified.

I glance down at the pilfered cushions and blankets that line the floor underneath the clothes rail. My cheeks feel like they are on fire. How could I have forgotten that he would see it if I opened the door?

"I... I don't like to sleep where I work," I try to say casually. I don't know if I have pulled it off.

Behind me the huge bed festooned in bright red silk sheets seems to glower at me. Taunting and mocking and disgruntled at my rejection.

Brodie clears his throat. "That makes sense."

He understands? He doesn't think I'm crazy? That... that gives me butterflies. Not only can he follow my logic, I can't sense any condemnation from him. No disgust. This lovely man has just been confronted with the reality of me being a sex worker and he still likes me.

I swallow uneasily. Why do I still call myself a sex worker? It's time to accept reality and stop denying the truth. Sex workers can leave if they want to. I haven't been able to leave for a long time. I'm a slave. Nothing more than property. The very thing I never wanted to be, and the very reason I ran away from my pack.

Seems like fate is a bitch.

Now I'm just standing with my back to Brodie, staring at my clothes like I've fully lost my mind.

"Oh! Sorry! I'll let you get dressed." says Brodie.

I hear him step towards the door and my heart lurches.

"No wait! Just turn your back please, I won't be long. I'd... um like some company."

A painfully long silence stretches out. Did I sound too needy? Is he going to flee?

"Sure," he says calmly.

Hiding my huff of relief, I quickly grab a set of clothes and start trying to wriggle into them. It's far more awkward than I would like but that's what I get for not drying off. Clothes stick to damp skin. I know this. There is no point in getting flustered about it. But logic isn't helping me here, and hopping around like this is absurd. Why did I even make Brodie turn around? It's not as if nobody has ever seen me naked before. I'm not shy about my body, I know I lucked out genetically.

But I don't want Brodie to see me like that. As just a hot body. I want him to keep seeing me, the person. Which means, my seduction plan will not work. I don't want Brodie's body. I don't want to have him in a shallow and meaningless way. I want him. All of him.

Shit.

This crush is bad.

Finally, I'm dressed. My hair is probably looking all disheveled but I can't ignore Brodie while I get my straighteners out. So instead, I walk over to the small two-seater table by my window.

"Come have a seat," I say.

Brodie walks over and sits down. He looks out of the window for a brief moment, appreciating the view, no doubt. Then his attention is back fully on me. As if I'm the most interesting thing in the world.

"Would you like a drink?" I ask.

I have a mini fridge in my room. I rarely use it and I can't for the life of me remember what is in it.

"A soda would be great, thanks."

I should have one of those. I flash him a smile and walk over to the fridge. All I have to do is fetch him a drink, sit down and act normal. It shouldn't be too hard. So why does it feel like the hardest challenge of my life?

Chapter Eleven

Brodie

I can say one thing for billionaires, they get to have some damn nice stuff. This treadmill is great. It's so smooth and quiet. And the view is spectacular. The treadmill is placed right up to a floor to ceiling window. I'm running, and all of London is spread out before me in the warm afternoon light. I can see the Thames, the Houses of Parliament. Trafalgar Square. And beyond them, the bustling capital continues to spread out, all the way to the horizon.

It would look great at night. All sparkling lights radiating out as far as the eye can see. Maybe I could bring Red here? With a picnic.

A laugh threatens to overtake me, which wouldn't be a good idea while I'm running this fast. I'll fall flat on my face and get thrown off of the treadmill. But my stupid idea deserves to be laughed at. A date in a gym? In the dark? Where the hell did that thought come from? It's hardly romantic, and I'm sure Red is used to the view. And why oh why am I assuming he would want to go on a date with me in the first place? Talk about ego.

Sitting in his room, drinking a can of Coke may have been the most enjoyable hour of my life in a long time. It doesn't mean he feels the same. For all I know I could have bored the poor man to tears and he was merely politely pretending to be interested in what I was saying.

Come to think of it, what had I waffled about for that long? Tales from my army days most likely. It tends to be my go to when I'm nervous. Oh, my god. I probably made a right idiot of myself.

The lights above me start to flash like a crazy disco, but it's not the pattern that I've come to learn signifies Smithson's arrival.

"Annie, what is the notification?"

The virtual assistant chirps for a moment. "An unaccompanied guest is arriving."

Oh. What's the protocol for that? Do the boys still need to assemble on the stage? I'm assuming that an unaccompanied guest means that Smithson has granted someone access to his harem, but he hasn't got time to attend with them.

I stop the treadmill, grab my towel and head off to the party area while wiping sweat off of my face. By the time I arrive, half the boys are already here. The others hurry in as I take up my usual lurking spot.

Red flashes me a beautiful smile as he passes me, and my heart does a strange flip. Arrhythmia. It's just a spell of arrhythmia, it has to be. I should run a heart scan on myself.

Ian strolls in, chatting away amicably to the guest, who appears to be a tall, nondescript man in a dark gray suit. He looks late thirties and yet again I don't recognize him from my research on the rich and famous. Just who is Smithson sharing his harem out to? Knowledge of the paranormal world must be contained, for everyone's safety.

Ian and the guest walk past me without seeming to notice me, which is great. Then the man's feet stop a few paces from the stage. I hate to empathize with the creep, but seeing all the boys together would fry anyone's brain. He stands stock still, his back is to me so I can't see his expression, but I can imagine.

The silence stretches for a long moment. Red has his usual position at the front and he is standing with his hip cocked at an alluring angle, while he stares at the stranger with come-to-bed eyes.

I know why he is doing it and hugely respect his willingness to protect his friends. But I hate it. He doesn't owe me a thing. We are barely friends, and even if we were more, that wouldn't make him my property. His body would always be his to do with as he pleases. But I still hate it. I still want to smash the stranger's head in for even looking at Red.

"Yellow," says the man.

Relief surges through me quickly followed by guilt. Lello's smile falters for a moment and he looks devastated, but he soon recovers and beams at the visitor. He steps nimbly off of the stage, takes the stranger by the hand and leads him to his room. I watch them go with a heavy heart. My guts feel full of lead. I can't stand this.

Blindly I stagger away. I need to be alone because I can't possibly hide my emotions. They are too raw, too powerful. This is going to have to be my last mission, I can't do this anymore. I can't bottle everything away.

It feels like it takes forever to reach my room. And once I do, it offers little solace. Shower. I need to get into the shower. Then I can scream, punch the wall, cry. As well as wash all my workout sweat away.

Throwing my clothes on the floor as I go, I hurry into the shower. The hit of the hot spray feels good. With the sound of the water shielding me, I allow the strangled cry stuck in my throat to come out. Poor Lello. Anyone having to have sex with someone they don't want to is abhorrent. But Lello is bonded to Smithson. Every part of him will be recoiling in repulsion. And the cruelty is so avoidable. Smithson didn't need to bite him. He doesn't need to offer him to others, he has six other boys for that. He didn't need to hunt him with a net and abduct him from his home in the first place. The man is a billionaire, it is not like he is going to have any problems getting laid.

He is just a sadistic bastard. And I really hope the Council decides to assassinate him. I've never met anyone who deserves murder more. It would be extra nice if they assign the task to me. I'd get a hell of a lot of satisfaction out of it.

Okay, I need to breathe. Deep, even breaths. I need to let this rage go, it's not going to help anything and I need my wits about me before I ruin everything.

Slowly, ever so slowly, I feel my normal equilibrium come back. I'm in control of myself once again. I tell the shower to stop, grab a towel and head towards my bedroom.

I'm just putting on a pair of black sweats, when Red bursts in through my door.

"Lello has been hurt!" he exclaims.

His eyes are wide and frantic. His breathing is rapid. I'm running out of the door before I've had time to process a single thought. In the hallway I see Ian frog marching the guest away. The overseer has the man's arm twisted behind his back as well as holding a fistful of his hair.

"You fucking piece of shit!" snarls Ian.

Suddenly I like the overseer a lot more than I did. But there is no time to ponder that. I run to Lello's room. Pink, Ned and Jade are crowded around the bed. Lello is laying naked on his front and whimpering. What I can see of his face is horrendously bruised. All deep purple and his eye is swollen shut.

"I did everything he said!" he sobs, and the bewildered confusion in his voice is breaking my heart.

Red runs in with my kit bag. I'm glad one of us still has their wits about him. I take it with a nod of thanks.

"Lello, sweetie, can you roll over so I can see where you are hurt?" I say as gently as I can.

He just continues to sob. I glance up at Ned, who is standing on the other side of the bed from me. He nods his understanding, places a hand gently on Lello's shoulder and carefully rolls him over. Lello gasps and whines but doesn't resist. As soon as his abdomen is revealed, my attention is drawn to the dark bruises there. Fucking hell. The bastard really did a number on him.

"Where does it hurt the most, Lello?" I ask. I need to know where to start.

"Inside!" he wails.

My eyebrows rise. I was not expecting that.

"He used a cock sleeve and it was really big," Lello sobs.

Oh crap, that doesn't sound good. I start looking around for it. I highly doubt that Ian allowed the bastard to pack it away before he dragged him out, so it has to be here somewhere. Red catches on to what I am doing and starts searching too.

"Here," he says as he pokes something on the floor with his foot.

I lean over to look. It is huge. And covered with huge bumps and ridges. It looks like a torture device, not something built for pleasure.

Oh fuck. Lello could have some serious internal damage. Paranormal healing is going to be far better than anything I can do with bandages and ointments.

"We need to take him to his pool. Water will help him heal," I say to Ned, before remembering that it's daytime and the vampire won't be able to carry him outside. My gaze flicks to Jade. Do fey have supernatural strength?

Jade gives me a worried glance. Fine, I'll have to carry him. Lello doesn't know me but it will have to do. I scoop him up and stand up. He weighs nothing, he is a tiny little scrap of a thing. How could anyone do this to him?

I stride towards the roof terrace. Lello's little entourage trotting along anxiously by my side. Lello doesn't seem distressed in my arms, thankfully. Perhaps nothing will ever break his trusting nature. And I'm not sure how to feel about that.

Ned stops dead at the doorway and I feel bad for him. He clearly cares a lot for his friend and it sucks he can't come with us.

The pool has large shallow roman steps into it, so I step down onto the first one. Fuck, that's cold. It's barely above my ankle and it's biting. I think it might not be merely unheated, but actually chilled. Scottish lochs are deep and not known for warmth.

Suddenly Blue is by my side. He is naked and water is streaming off of his slender body. He has clearly just run over from his salty pool.

He holds out his arms and gestures for me to give him Lello. Of course, freezing cold water won't bother him at all and he will be able to go under with Lello, which will be even better than merely submerging. Sirens need salt water, but being in fresh water for a few hours won't do Blue any harm.

Carefully, I hand Lello over. The little kelpie whimpers and then snuggles into Blue's chest. It seems that he is happier with someone he knows and trusts. I'm glad he does actually have some survival instincts.

Blue walks into the water, going deeper and deeper until they are under the surface. There is nothing more I can do right now. I'll ask Blue to bring him back up in an hour so I can check Lello's healing progress. Until then. I'm just useless. Useless and standing out here bare chested because I was only half dressed when Red came to fetch me.

It shouldn't make me feel uncomfortable but it does. It makes me feel exposed when I already feel like all my emotions are laid bare. My feelings are naked. Unprotected. Clear for anyone to see.

I was upset about Lello being fucked against his will and that was before the guy turned out to be an evil jerk and violently beat the little kelpie for no reason at all. Just because he got some twisted kick out of it.

But I'm not supposed to care. I'm meant to be an asshole. Someone who took this job for the perks. Perks that surely everyone has started to notice I haven't used.

"I'll come back later to see how he is," I say gruffly before striding away back towards my room. Even through all my storming emotions and twisting thoughts, I can feel the weight of Red's gaze on my back and it is so hard not to turn around and look at him.

I want to know what he is thinking. I want him to know that I'm not really an asshole. I want him to like me. And that's becoming a huge problem, because I'm starting to want that, more than I want my mission to succeed.

I'm going to have to do something about it.

Chapter Twelve

Red

I'm just dishing up the pasta I cooked for dinner, when Brodie walks in. He has dark circles under his eyes and he looks haggard.

"How is Lello?" I ask.

"Tucked up in his bed and healing well," he answers.

I let out a little sigh of relief. That's great news. And I'm going to take the happiness it gives me. I've learned to cling onto all the small wins. To find joy where I can. It's the only way to nurture the strength to carry on.

Ned grabs one of the bowls of pasta and walks up to Brodie with it.

"Is it okay for Lello to eat this?" he asks.

Brodie nods, "Yes, food will be good for him."

The vampire says nothing and just strides out of the kitchen with the pasta. Brodie doesn't seem to mind the rudeness. He just takes a seat at the table.

"Do you want some pasta?" I ask.

"Yes, please."

Please. Such a small simple word and so lovely to hear. It makes me feel all warm and gooey inside. The boys are all polite to me, most of the time. Well, Ned is usually grumpy, but that is just who he is. Anyway, politeness from Brodie just hits differently. It is a sure sign that I really do have it bad.

I hand him a bowl and take a seat across from him. Pink and Jade are already tucking in so with no further preamble I dive into eating too. We eat in companionable silence for a while. The clink of cutlery against bowls is the only sound.

"Red, can you come to my room at nine tonight please?" says Brodie.

The sudden silence is deafening. Pink's fork is frozen halfway to his mouth and Jade has gone stiller than a statue.

"Why?" I ask hesitantly.

Brodie's gaze is fixed on his food. "Why do you think?" he snaps gruffly.

I feel my brows furrowing in confusion. What has got into him? I know he is not like this. I've never been more bewildered in my life. My gaze flicks to Jade and Pink, who both give me pitying looks before resuming their meals.

Slowly, I do the same. Brodie has every right to order me to his room and to demand services. All the staff are allowed to do so. But I'm just so sure he is not like that. Am I misunderstanding what he is asking? Is he up to something? Or have I built a silly little fantasy in my head of what he is like and I don't actually know the man at all? It's a depressing thought.

I guess I'll be finding out the answers to these questions at nine. Carefully I hide my frustrated sigh. I can just tell that it's going to be a long evening.

It's precisely nine P.M but I can't stand the suspense anymore.
I need to get it over and done with. If Brodie does just want to
fuck, at least I will know. I will be able to extinguish my silly little
crush. And besides, even if he is actually an asshole, he is still a
damn good-looking one. Having sex with him won't be the end
of the world.

I walk into his room and shut the door behind me. Brodie
is standing frozen in the middle of the room, facing the blank
wall. I think he was pacing the room and I have caught him
mid-stride. The look he shoots me is frantic and his hair is all
over the place. Has he been pulling on it?

"Red... I'm so sorry!" he says. "I should never have talked to
you like that at dinner."

I shrug and try to keep my face blank. It's nice that he is trying
to apologize but I still don't have a clue what is going on or what
he wants with me.

He sees that I'm waiting for him to explain and he flushes
before dropping his gaze.

"I... er... am impotent and I don't want anyone to know, so if
you could just stay awhile and pretend... I'd really appreciate it."

He looks up at me and the look in his wide eyes is one of
pain, confliction and torment. He is not telling me the truth,
or at least not the whole truth, and he is feeling distressed over
it. What a mystery. It's intriguing and I do like a puzzle.

"Okay," I say carefully.

His eyebrows shoot up in surprise, "Really?"

"Hanging out here isn't a hardship and I don't mind telling people you fucked me." I say.

His shoulders sag in relief and the pain etched on his face eases.

"As long as I can say you have a tiny dick and don't know how to use it," I add.

He barks out a laugh. A rich, deep laugh that seems to dance along my skin and leave goose pimples behind.

"Seems fair enough," he agrees with a wry smile.

I smile back at him. See I was right all along. He is a nice person. There is no way in hell that a toxic man would find my comment funny. A bad man would be furious at the mere suggestion of that rumor. I have no idea why he is pretending to be something he is not, but something instinctual and deep within me is telling me to trust that he has his reasons and to roll with it.

"Would you like a drink?" offers Brodie.

"Sure," I smile.

I take a seat on his small sofa as he rummages in his mini-fridge. It gives me a perfect view of his gorgeous ass as he bends over. The muscle tone in those well-defined glutes! I bet he can pound away for hours. Quickly, I look away before I can have any more filthy thoughts and before he catches me ogling him.

Is he really impotent? And in what way? There are a million ways to have fun. I sure as hell wouldn't mind exploring all of them to find something that we both enjoy.

Wow! Did that thought really just cross my mind? I'm such a creep. And I can't believe that part of me is a little disappointed that I'm not here to be railed.

"What would you like?" he asks.

To climb into bed with you.

"Orange juice, please. With vodka." I manage to say, because he is talking about drinks and nothing more.

He laughs again. "A man after my own heart."

I watch him as he finishes with the fridge and walks over to the drinks cabinet. Only staff get those in their room. I wonder if he knows how lucky he is.

He returns with drinks, hands one to me and then to my delight, squeezes onto the small sofa next to me. His thigh is pressing against mine and the sensation makes me ache for more. I want to feel him all over me.

I take a sip of my drink and the pleasant burn of the alcohol is a poor substitute for the pleasure I'm sure Brodie's hands on me would ignite. My desire for him is becoming incessant. It was dampened for a few hours after dinner while angst and anxiety spiraled through me, taunting me with the thought that Brodie might not be all that I hoped. But now that my hope has been restored, it seems my desire has returned. This time with the intensity of a thousand burning suns.

"Your dancing is incredible, how did you learn?" asks Brodie.

"Practice," I say and then wince inwardly. The poor man is trying to make conversation and I'm shutting him down.

I take a deep breath, put my drink down, and continue. "I ran away from my pack when I was a young teenager. I came to

London with no human birth certificate, no National Insurance number. My career options were limited."

"So you became a dancer?"

I nod.

"Is that how Smithson found you?"

I nod again. "He asked me to be his live-in sugar baby. I was thrilled. I thought I could continue to pretend to be human, but I went into heat... and that's how he found out about the paranormal world."

Silence. Still and awkward. My confession hangs awkwardly between us. Exposing the paranormal world to mundanes is a crime that the Council sometimes punishes by death.

"This is all my fault," I whisper. Clarifying my guilt, but damn does it feel good to say it out loud.

Brodie twists around to face me, but I look away in shame. His gentle fingers take my chin and coax me back to meeting his gaze.

"This is no one's fault but Smithson's," he says determinedly.

Stupid tears start to fill my eyes, so I blink them away. Suddenly, soft gentle lips are on mine. Brodie is kissing me, feather soft.

I kiss him back. Eagerly. Hungrily. Desperately. He feels so good. Tastes so divine. I ease my tongue into his mouth and he moans. My arms wrap around his neck and I slide onto his lap, like a moth drawn to a flame.

His hands caress my shoulders, but then he is pushing me away. Off of his lap, away from his lips. He stares at me but I can't read the look in his eyes.

"Sorry," he mutters.

His fingers rise up and trace his lips as if he is chasing the feel of me.

"I think you have been here long enough to be convincing," he says.

I climb to my feet. I know a dismissal when I hear one. But this one hurts a hell of a lot more than any other I have ever received. Somehow I make it across his room and out of the door. I can feel his gaze on my back the whole way. Just as I had felt his very large and very hard manhood when I was sitting on his lap.

Whatever the hell is going on, I really don't think there is anything wrong with his cock.

Chapter Thirteen

Brodie

Last night I kissed Red. It's early afternoon now and the thought has been going around my head all day. No matter how many times I say it to myself, it still doesn't seem real. It feels like a dream and I can't decide if it was a nightmare.

He felt so good in my arms. The press of his warm, lithe body against my chest had been divine. He tasted so sweet and the sensation of his soft lips against my own, had lit fireworks off in my mind. It was the best kiss of my life. No contest. But I shouldn't have been kissing him at all.

I should have stuck to my original plan. Play my part. Keep my cover. Order Red to my room and fuck him like it means nothing. Get over my dangerous desire.

That stupid whiny part of me that thought that Red thinking badly of me would be the most awful catastrophe in the world? That part of me I should have ignored.

The panic I had felt as I waited for him had been intense. The regret I had felt for talking to him like that, had nearly brought me to my knees. It had all seemed so insurmountable. Telling him the truth would put him in danger. Going through with it would make him hate me forever. Both options were hell.

My idea of claiming to be impotent had been a stroke of genius. An excuse. A reason. It could make me still an asshole, but with the hope that Red would not hate me forever for it.

And then I'd gone and kissed him.

I'm such an idiot and now I'm back to square one. An unhealthy obsession on Red that is a risk to the mission.

But at least everyone else is going to think I fucked him. I've solved that problem for now. No more suspicion about why I'm not taking any advantages of the perks. And the way I chucked Red out of my room? He is definitely going to believe I am an asshole.

So I have made progress. There is no need to want to lie in bed all day moping like a broken hearted teenager. I am a professional after all.

And talking about being a professional, it's time to go check on Lello. I've managed to avoid Red so far today, hopefully I can continue to do so. I head out of my room. I've already checked on the little kelpie a few times today and he is healing really well. Thank heavens for paranormal strength. I just hope his mind is as resilient.

As I reach his daffodil yellow door, I think about knocking. But no one knocks here, so I walk in. The room is dark and it takes a moment for my eyes to adjust.

The very first thing I notice is that Red is here. Awareness of him jolts like electricity through every cell of my body. I see him. I swear I can hear his breathing. I'm pretty sure I can smell him.

And I can just sense him in some unidentifiable six sense way. His presence consumes me.

Slowly, ever so slowly my mind starts to register what else it can see.

All the boys, apart from Gray, are sitting on the bed, watching the giant television screen that is the only source of light in the room. Those are some damn good blackout blinds.

Lello is sat in the middle, resting against the headboard, amongst a sea of pillows. His friends are all sprawled around him. I can make out popcorn and sweets in the flickering light.

Huge bouquets of flowers festoon every corner and line every wall of the room. Smithson sent flowers? What a sick fuck. Make someone besotted with you, pimp them out and then send fucking flowers when they get brutally beaten? What an utter bastard. The very worst thing about it is that it's probably going to work on Lello's poor addled mind. It's going to keep him as infatuated as ever.

A scream sounds out from the screen and they all jump. Lello than giggles. A horror film then. I walk towards the bed. Ned glances at me.

"Shh!" he demands.

Everyone else is transfixed on the film. I don't think they have even seen me. Red is sitting to the left of Lello and there is a tiny bit of bed left on the edge. Should I squeeze in and join them? Am I welcome? Or would I be intruding? Hesitantly, I take a step forward.

Red doesn't tear his eyes away from the screen but he pats the tiny space next to him. Clearly gesturing for me to join him.

Dazedly I do as I am told. Sneaking in and trying not to disturb anyone.

The bed is very comfortable. And the feel of Red's thigh pressed against mine, is giving me déjà vu from last night. Determinedly, I fix my attention on the film. A young girl is walking anxiously down a long dark corridor in a very haunted looking house.

The music ramps up and Lello squeals. In front of me, Ned squirms. It makes me smile. I'm watching a horror film with a vampire, and several other paranormals and they are just as scared as me and Pink. It's hilarious and adorable.

The music gets even more intense as the young girl approaches a truly terrifying door. I have no idea what's going on, but it's very clear to me that she should not open it.

Red's hand slips into mine and holds on tightly. Suddenly it feels as if a whole swarm of butterflies have taken up residence in my stomach. I'm being ridiculous. Red is just scared, that is all. I'm the closest person to grab onto. It doesn't mean anything.

His hand is warm and so much smaller than mine. I never want to let him go. Besides, it would be rude to snatch my hand back in the middle of a horror film.

It's fine. It's all fine. I'm sitting in the dark holding the hand of a wolf shifter who is scared of a ghost film. I should think about how amusing that is. Not how the feel of his touch is making my heart beat faster. Not how I'm holding the hand of someone I'm trying desperately not to fall in love with.

I'm going to just sit here, hold his hand for as long as he will let me, and the only thing I am going to think about is the movie. Nothing else is going to cross my mind. Nothing else at all.

It's going to be great.

Chapter Fourteen

Red

I can still feel the echo of Brodie's hand in my own. Sitting in the dark, holding his hand and feeling the heat of his body seep into me from where our legs were pressed together, had been the happiest hour of my life in a very long time.

I need to rationalize it though. Brodie is a big, strong man. My instincts are probably thinking alpha, even though he is human. I've been scared and stressed for years, so of course the allure of an alpha taking care of me and fixing all my problems is going to be irresistible.

It would be heavenly if my only responsibility was to submit to another. Another who would keep me safe and care for me. Make all the right decisions.

A wistful sigh escapes from me and echoes around my empty room. Sitting in the dark holding his hand felt so amazing because it gave my instincts hope.

That's all it was. I'm not actually falling in love. How could I? I barely know the man. And even if I was, I'm sure he is not feeling the same way. He probably just believed my ruse that I was scared of the film and he is nice enough not to snatch his hand away.

Chucking me out of his room after kissing me, wasn't very nice. But I know he had his reasons. I know there is something bigger going on. He is a nice person at heart. Or perhaps I'm just far too soft. Whatever it is, it seems I have forgiven him. I'm not angry about it. I just want him to kiss me again.

"Ned? Ned!" Lello's distraught wail is clear through the wall that divides my room from the vampire's.

I'm up in a flash and in his room in a heartbeat. Ned is on the bed, lying on his back, motionless. Far too still.

"He won't wake up!" sobs Lello as he tugs on Ned's hand.

"Go get Brodie!" I snap.

Lello flashes me a wide-eyed look before dashing off as if the hounds of hell are on his heels.

The blackout curtains are down. The sun has just set. Ned is less nocturnal than other vampires thanks to the special glass in the penthouse and his desire to be in sync with the rest of us. But he should be waking up now. Is that the problem? Has he been keeping an unnatural rhythm for too long?

Desperately, I run my gaze over him, trying to see if there is anything I can do. He looks pale. He looks dead. He is dead, I remind myself. Did he go to sleep and whatever magic resurrects vampires just left? Didn't ignite?

I'm going to be sick, this is awful.

Brodie runs in with Lello right behind him and I have never been more relieved in my life. The healer quickly examines Ned as I wait with bated breath.

"It's parva mors," he pronounces after what feels like forever.

I stare at Brodie in alarm. I have no idea what that is, but it doesn't sound good.

"It's like cot death for young vampires. Sometimes they go to sleep and don't revive," he explains.

I swallow painfully. "He is dead, dead?"

Lello gasps, but I can't focus on him right now. Every part of me is fixed on the healer. There has to be something he can do. There just has to be. Brodie won't give up, will he?

Brodie doesn't answer me. He is too busy moving quickly and efficiently. He fetches a scalpel from his bag and with no hesitation, neatly cuts his wrist. I watch, transfixed as he holds his cut over Ned's slightly parted mouth and lets his blood drip into the vampire.

"If it's not been too long, human blood can bring him back," explains Brodie.

My heart flutters. Brodie isn't wasting time by getting Ian to bring a human. The healer is willing to feed Ned himself in an effort to save him. He cares that much. Brodie is going to do everything he can to save a vampire he barely knows. I hope it is enough. It has to be enough. Ned can't just cease to exist.

I watch the vampire's motionless body and try to bring him back to life with the force of my will. As if I think that will do anything. But I have to try, and it's the only thing I have to offer. I'd gladly give my blood too, but human blood is better for vampires. Even I know that.

Suddenly, with absolutely no warning, Ned moves and I nearly jump out of my skin. The vampire's eyes snap open to reveal a glowing feral red. His hands grab Brodie's arm and yank it down to his mouth. His jaw moves as he bites down onto the human's flesh. Brodie swears and flinches but he stands steady. It doesn't look like he is trying to get away.

The vampire sucks noisily and greedily. I can see his throat moving as he swallows Brodie's blood.

The tension in the air is palpable. Ned is awake now, does that mean he is going to be okay? Is Brodie now the one in danger? Have the tables turned so dramatically?

"Get him off me," groans Brodie softly.

Lello and I both jump forward to start trying to prise them apart, but it is Lello's soft, "No Ned! Stop!" that causes the vampire to free Brodie.

The healer staggers back a couple of steps. Then he retrieves a white cloth from his pocket and presses it against his wrist.

Ned sits up. The red feral light from his eyes has gone. He looks like himself. Lello jumps onto his lap and throws his arms around him. Ned hugs him back but his attention is fixed on Brodie. I can almost see the vampire putting together the puzzle pieces and figuring out what just happened.

"You taste good, human," he drawls.

Brodie snorts in derision. "Onetime offer, old man."

Ned licks his lips, "Shame."

"Fuck you," mutters Brodie.

My gaze flicks between the two of them. They are acting like a pair of alphas. All bristles and insults, but I can sense affection between them. I'm pretty sure the correct translation of their exchange was something like 'Thanks for saving my life.' 'You're welcome.'

Some people have the strangest way of communicating. But hey, as long as it works.

Abruptly, my attention is caught by a strange scent coming off of Brodie. Then suddenly, he staggers past me and out the door. Leaving his kit bag behind. With my heart hammering in alarm, I chase after him, only to find him just outside Ned's door, leaning heavily on the wall in the hallway. He only made it a few steps. His eyes are glassy and his face flushed. He seems dazed and completely out of it. Did Ned take too much blood? What should I do?

Realization hits me. Oh shit, yes, I remember now. Vampire bites make people incredibly horny. Something in their saliva acts like a drug. The strange smell is Brodie's intense, artificially induced arousal. My gaze drops down to his crotch. Yep, that's a very big bulge.

Wow! My head is spinning. A mere moment ago I thought one of my friends was going to die permanently. Now I'm standing in a hallway with my very aroused crush. The sudden change is dizzying, but I must say I'm much more a fan of this situation than the first one.

Not the least because this is a situation I can help with. I know exactly what to do and I'm very happy to do it. With that thought in mind, I spring into action.

Gently, I take his hand and lead him the few faltering steps to my room. Once inside, I turn back to face him. He stares back at me in bewildered confusion. He doesn't understand why I have brought him here.

"Let me take care of that for you," I explain, tilting my head towards his erection.

It's the least I can do after he saved Ned's life, and besides, it's the perfect excuse to get exactly what I want. Brodie in my bed. I had dismissed the idea of just having sex with him as not being enough, but it seems I'm backtracking on that decision. My desire for him is just too strong. I want him in any way I can have him.

He stares at me hazily for a moment. I stare back. It feels as if we are the only two people in the world. Like the universe itself is holding its breath, waiting for Brodie's decision. Then Brodie licks his lips and nods.

My heart does a flip, and my stomach does a cartwheel as a dizzying wave of excited adrenaline surges through me.

Finally.

Finally, I get to have Brodie.

Chapter Fifteen

Red

I drop to my knees in front of Brodie. His eyes darken as he looks down at me. I feel the heat of his gaze on my skin. He wants me. He needs me. His hunger for me is absolute. Knowing that, gives me a rush like no other. It's the very best feeling in the world.

Holding his gaze steadily, I reach out and unbutton his jeans. My fingers work nimbly. I'm a professional at freeing cocks. I have enough experience to make it look effortless, graceful even. I wish my life hadn't taken a path that taught me these skills, but now that I have them, I'm going to use them to give Brodie the time of his life. I want to rock his world. Make him never forget me. Ruin him for all others. It is the one way I can make him mine.

His cock springs free, full, heavy and beautiful. I wet my lips. Keeping my eyes locked on his, I stick out my tongue and give his cock a long lick all the way along the underneath, from root to crown. His salty, musky taste floods my mouth and I moan.

His entire body shudders and I exult in the power I have over him. His desire for me is intoxicating. I take a deep breath as if I can breathe it in. My hands find the back of his muscular thighs. My tongue starts to toy with the tip of his cock. I want to swallow him whole, and feel the weight of him on my tongue, stretching my mouth wide, but all good things come to those who wait.

I swirl my tongue around the head of his cock and am rewarded with his deep groan and a burst of pre-cum. He tastes good. I can't wait to drink down his full release. I hum my pleasure and he throws back his head and gasps. He has broken our locked gaze, but I don't mind.

I start bobbing my head, taking more of him with each glide of my lips. He shudders again. Strong fingers run through my hair, I tense for a moment but he doesn't take control, just softly cards my hair. It feels wonderful.

I relax my throat and slide all the way down, taking him all. He is well endowed and my pride tells me it's probably the first time anybody has taken all of him. No one else has been able to do this for him. I am the first to give him this glorious sensation. The groan he gives me in return is music to my ears. I swallow around him, milking him with my throat and he yells as he peaks, shooting hot wet gushes down my throat.

I moan in satisfaction and then pull off of him so I can breathe. I look up at him. His eyes are closed, he is all flushed and breathing heavily. My gaze flicks down to his still hard cock. Damn, vampire venom really is something.

Suddenly, I'm bouncing on my back on the bed. A yelp of surprise escapes me. Brodie looms over me, his eyes dark with lust. I think he is deciding what to do to me. But then he pauses, and I can see the inner battle written all over his face.

"Can I eat you?" he bites out.

My heart swells along with my cock. He is fighting vampire venom to ask consent. That's some will power. I nod hastily, I don't want to keep him waiting. I don't want to keep myself waiting.

His hands find the waistband of my flimsy trousers and he slowly slides them off my hips. Then down and down my legs, until they are off. He throws them over his shoulder, his eyes roaming over my near naked body as if he is drinking in the sight, committing it to memory.

I'd like to take this stupid top off. It is barely covering my nipples, but I still want it gone. I want to be naked before him, I want him to see all of me. But I don't want to move. Something in his gaze seems to pin me to the spot.

"Hold on to the headboard," he rasps.

Wordlessly my arms float up above my head and I grasp the headboard tightly. His strong hands rest on my inner thighs and gently spread my legs apart. He lowers himself down until he is lying on his stomach on the bed, his head nestled between my spread legs.

Warm, wet heat laps at my hole, and I squeal. Pleasure blossoms instantly, a low intense heat in my gut. That one lick felt incredible. He is going to destroy me. And I'm going to love it.

He licks again and I all but howl. He chuckles and starts twirling around and around my rim, sending euphoria shooting like electricity throughout my entire body. That feels so damn good. I feel a gush of slick leave me and I tense. Brodie is human, is he going to think slick is gross?

He groans hungrily and starts lapping in earnest, as if he can't get enough of the taste of me. I sigh in bliss and sink back into the mattress. He doesn't mind slick at all.

He flicks over and over my hole until I'm whining and my hips are desperate to buck, but his firm hands hold me in place so that I can do nothing but ride the waves of pleasure that he is sending crashing through my entire being.

The very tip of his hot tongue enters me, and I yowl. I would have levitated off of the bed if it were not for his firm grip. I tighten my hold on the headboard and prepare to hold on for dear life.

He pushes his soft wet tongue into me. Spreading the soft flesh inside apart. Penetrating me. Taking my body and making it his own. His tongue stiffens and starts to work in and out. Thrusting. He is fucking me with his tongue and the warm wet glide passing over and over my rim causes a delicious friction that build and builds. A tingling starts deep within me, it intensifies and spreads, flowing outwards until it consumes every cell in my body. My mind alights with sparks of sheer joy, my back arches as all my muscles quiver with ecstasy. My cock spurts warm wetness onto my stomach.

But Brodie shows me no mercy. He continues to work me with his tongue, adding the occasional swirl to the thrusts. As an omega I'm very sensitive down there anyway, but now? Still riding the aftershocks of a tremendous orgasm? The sensations are overwhelming. So intense I feel like they are catapulting me to another reality.

I'm whimpering non-stop now, my legs are trying to close but he is holding me down and spread and licking and licking and licking until I'm thrown into another orgasm. This one even more intense than the last. I see stars, hell I see time and feel sound. And I don't drift down because Brodie still has his tongue buried in my ass. He is deeper now, as far as he can reach. Caressing the soft sides of my channel that haven't received any direct attention yet and now those nerve endings are singing with joy, adding their delight to my already full nervous system.

Suddenly he stops and I take the opportunity to wheeze in a breath.

"I think you can give me one more, kitten," he all but growls.

His tongue dives right back into me. I can feel my eyes rolling back in my head. His soft lips settle around my rim and rub it softly as his tongue continues to work me. This time I howl and sob as I peak, his tongue flick and flicks, each tingling jolt whipping my orgasm along, fueling the fire that is raging through me until it feels like I'm going to be riding this crest forever.

The intensity mixes pleasure with pain. I can feel tears on my cheeks. My throat is sore from my screams and still the pleasure rolls on and on.

Dizziness swarms through me and I'm floating in a warm sea of bliss. Everything is black and peaceful. There is nothing here but joy.

"Red?" Brodie sounds concerned.

Blearily I open my eyes. He is staring down at me. I feel as boneless as an overcooked noodle. I couldn't move if the bed was on fire. I feel fuzzy. Content. Sated.

"I think you passed out for a moment there? Are you okay?"

I try to smile but my muscles are too lax to coordinate. "Hmm mm," I try instead. I'm fine. I'm more than fine. I've never been better. I have no idea if I managed to convey that with the contented sound that was all I was able to make.

My eyelids are drooping. Sleep would be lovely, I could float on the bliss for longer and have wonderful dreams. Just as I'm drifting off I feel Brodie plant a soft kiss on my forehead and I finally manage a smile.

Life is good.

Chapter Sixteen

Brodie

I never should have left Red like that. Okay, I was still out of it from the vamp venom and feeling overwhelmed, but eating someone's ass until they pass out, and then just tucking them up and running away, is an awful thing to do to a person.

He must have been so pissed off at me when he woke up. I should have gone and apologized as soon as I came to my senses, instead of hiding in my room, but now it's lunchtime the next day and it feels as if I have left it far too long to say sorry now. I'm such an idiot.

But maybe it is for the best. A bit of vamp venom hasn't changed a thing. Red still needs to think I'm a jerk. I still can't blow my cover. Falling in love with him would still be a disaster.

Memories of last night flood through me yet again and I'm powerless to stop them. Red on his knees before me, looking up at me with his soft lips wrapped around my cock. Red writhing on the bed making the most beautiful noises of pleasure, as the taste of his slick consumed me.

The reality of Red in my arms was a thousand times better than all my fervent daydreams. I will never be able to get enough of him. I will never stop craving him, needing him.

My new image of heaven is where I get to bring Red to shuddering all-consuming orgasms over and over again. He is always beautiful, but when he peaks he is ethereal. A creature not meant for this world. I want to spend eternity worshiping him. He deserves no less.

The way he takes care of everyone? It's high time he was the one taken care of. He should be spoiled rotten and I should be the one doing it. I don't want him to ever have to worry about a single thing ever again.

I sigh heavily. Maybe after the mission is complete. Maybe then I can court him. It's something to hold onto at least, since it seems nothing is going to stop my infatuation. Telling myself I just have to wait, might work. Because telling myself, not ever, is seemingly impossible to accept. Hopefully, not right now, might just be bearable.

I sigh again. I'm supposed to be writing up notes, not fantasizing about Red. Forcing myself to focus on the tablet is hard, but I need to do it.

Slowly, I start typing about my concerns about Gray's muscle tone. He is kept chained to that bed all the time. I've put in a request for daily physiotherapy, but where Smithson's people are going to find a physiotherapist from, one that can handle a demon and keep quiet, I have no idea. I know the rudimentary basics so I'm going to have to start delivering that in the meantime. It will be far better than nothing.

Pink is no longer sore, the ointment I gave him helped, though I suspect it's more that no one has chosen him for a while. I'm worried about his mental health, but I don't think there is much I can do about that. Therapy while your life is a living hell is like trying to bail out the Titanic with a teaspoon. Once he is free from here, I hope youthful resilience will be on his side and enable him to heal. I'm not adding that to my notes, just my mental ones.

Lello has physically made a full recovery. He seems as bouncy as ever. I have no idea how much of that is a coping mechanism, or if it is a front he shows strangers like me, or if it genuinely is who he is as a person. Or even if his mind is completely addled by being bitten by Smithson. There is no way to tell, so I'm just going to have to focus on his physical health.

That leaves Ned to check on. He was supposed to be here half an hour ago. I guess I'm going to have to go find the stubborn ass.

I put the tablet down and head off in search of the vampire. I go to his room first and find him there, sprawled on his bed, reading a book.

"We had an appointment," I say.

Ned doesn't look up from his book. "I'm busy."

He is such a stubborn, belligerent ass. I really do like him.

"So you don't mind staying dead next time, old man?"

He drops his book and scowls at me. "I feel fine."

"I'm guessing you felt fine before it happened?"

Ned's scowl deepens. "I don't need you getting all sweaty and weird and begging me for another bite."

"Not going to happen. I told you, you aren't my type." I glare back at him. There is no way on earth I'm ever going to confess about the prophylactic I took against vamp venom addiction the very moment I staggered back to my room. Let him think it's the force of my own willpower.

"I've arranged for you to be fed more often, please don't be squeamish about it," I say.

"Go fuck yourself! I have no qualms about eating humans!"

I shrug and turn to walk away. "All good then."

I duck as the book comes sailing past my head. How sweet. Vampires have excellent aim. If he really wanted to hit me with it, he would have. He does like me. Grinning to myself, I stroll away.

Back in the med room, I pick up the tablet to enter Ned's notes and I see there is a message from Ian on the staff only message system. I click on it and then stagger into my chair.

Ian's message is just a string of the hot emoji, but the attachment is a video. It's Red sprawled over his bed while I'm eating him out. It's damn good quality for CCTV. I should have realized the boys would have cameras in their rooms. I'm going to have to check my room thoroughly.

The video plays on. I have a horrible feeling that if I click it, it will have sound too.

Red looks mesmerizing. He is so beautiful. A perfect femboy. All small and slender. The way his back is arching and the clear strain in his arms as he holds onto the headboard, short circuits my brain and goes straight to my dick. I can't stop watching as he spills gloriously and then tries to close his legs, but my rough, tanned hands, large against his smooth pale thighs, keep him spread open as I keep ravishing him. He bucks and wriggles delightfully and the look of tortured bliss on his face is going to make me cum in my pants.

I throw the tablet down. I should delete the video. But I know I won't. I should have stopped licking his hole once he became too sensitive. It doesn't look great on the consent front, now that I've seen it on film. And blaming it on the venom does not absolve me.

Fuck. I thought I only needed to apologize for running away afterwards. It seems I might need to apologize for everything. Including the unforgivable.

This is awful.

Chapter Seventeen

Red

Everyone thinks Lello is such a sweet little thing when actually he can be a right bossy little mare. Like right now. Demanding that we all play his favorite game with him. Hide and seek in the dark.

I wonder if he knows we all secretly enjoy it, even Ned, and that we all pretend to be just humoring him. If so, he is better at taking care of everyone than I am. The devious little so and so.

I grin fondly as I tiptoe down the dark hallway. This game must really suck for Pink and Brodie. The rest of us definitely have an advantage with our paranormal night vision. Especially Ned.

I'm shamelessly following Brodie's wonderful scent. Hiding in the dark somewhere with him is my idea of heaven. There are plenty of parts of the penthouse that don't have cameras. Which means, alone time, secret kisses and he will be able to hold me.

My feet pick up pace. I don't want to waste one precious second. I'm so busy tracking his scent that I'm not really paying attention to where I am going. So when I find him just outside Ian's office we both jump.

"Red!" he exclaims.

I lose myself in the depths of his beautiful eyes for a moment. "There are cameras in there. And motion sensors."

He holds my gaze steadily even though I'm pretty sure he can't see much of me at all in the dark.

"Just thought it would be a good place to hide," he says carefully.

"Of course," I agree easily.

He stares at me some more and the intensity makes the hairs on the back of my neck stand up. Surely he has to know I'm not a foe? I'm sure it is quite clear that I feel no loyalty to Ritchie. If Brodie is an agent from the Council, as I'm really starting to suspect, I'm fully on his side and willing to do whatever I can to help.

Though I suppose he wouldn't be a good agent if he trusted me just because we had some mind blowing make out sessions.

"I know a better place to hide," I say as I take his hand.

He lets me lead him up the hallway a little. I open a door that looks like it leads to a closet and pull Brodie in with me. Wires twist everywhere in a multitude of colors and an array of black boxes flash with little LED lights.

To fit in here with Brodie, we are having to stand pressed together. It would be chest to chest, except I barely come up to his shoulder. I ignore the intense distraction of having his wonderful body so close.

"This is the server room," I say casually. "No cameras in here. Always thought it would be a great place for a prank. If I knew what I was doing, I could access all the cameras, everything on the computer system. Make people's showers go crazy."

Brodie is staring at me again but this time I can feel his erection pressing against my stomach. So hopefully his thoughts are more along the lines of wanting to ravish me than deciding if I am a threat or not.

"I'm sorry!" he says suddenly.

My eyebrows rise in confusion. "For what?"

"The vamp venom. Leaving you." he trails off miserably.

I wrap my arms around his broad back and press my face against his chest. "It was hot as fuck, I loved every minute. And I know you couldn't stay and cuddle because of the cameras."

Brodie lets out a big sigh. Then he takes in a big breath and I think he is going to say something, but he doesn't. His arms wrap around me instead and he holds me tightly. I let out a little contented sigh. Being in Brodie's arms is bliss.

One of his hands moves up to my head and he gently strokes my hair. If I were a cat, I'd be purring. I don't even mind that he is messing my hair up. I could stay like this forever.

I tilt my head up to look at him and his soft lips claim my own. I moan into the kiss and melt into his body. I want to press every inch of myself against every inch of him. I don't want there to be a molecule between us.

Kissing Brodie is amazing. Just the feel of his lips has unleashed my lust. My cock is hard and my hole is wet. I want him. No, I need him. Poor man only kissed me and I am whimpering into his mouth and grinding into him like some feral beast.

His large, warm hands cup my ass, and I groan. I want more. Thankfully, he seems to read my urgency. His hand slips under the waistband of my trousers. His fingers drift down my crack, to my wet, needy hole and to my delight, he pushes two fingers inside of me. I break off our kiss to cry out in glee.

He fucks me with his fingers, fast and exquisitely while I just cling onto him and sob. He finds that special spot inside me and I see stars. My orgasm steals my breath, my sight, my everything, until the only thing I am aware of is Brodie.

I'm clenching around his fingers so tightly it sets off another wave of bliss. Brodie grunts softly and I scent his release. He came in his pants. Untouched. Just from fingering me. Man that is hot.

As I try to catch my breath, Brodie tidies us up as best he can. We definitely need to go clean up. I open the door and yelp in fright.

The lights are off but I can still clearly see that Lello is standing outside, arms crossed and tapping his foot.

"You're supposed to be playing hide and seek in the dark. Not sneaking off to have nooky. You can do that anytime."

"Sorry," I mumble.

Brodie mutters an apology too. Lello glares at us a moment longer before tossing his hair back over his shoulder and flouncing off.

"Shit," sighs Brodie.

"It's fine. You are supposed to be fucking me, remember?" I reassure. "And Lello will forgive us."

Brodie appears to ponder my words for a moment. Then he grins and I can't help but grin back.

"Nooky?" he questions with a raised eyebrow.

And I laugh. A very unsexy snort laugh, but Brodie doesn't seem to mind. His grin just intensifies until it is dazzling and all

I can think about is calculating how long it is going to be until I can next sneak off to have nooky with him.

I can't wait.

Chapter Eighteen

Brodie

I drift awake in confusion. My dream of being lost and alone in the mist is clinging onto me, making it hard to think. Slender arms are wrapped around me and a lithe body is pressed up to my back. A very naked body. It's Red, and he feels feverishly hot.

Alarmed, I turn around to face him. In the dim light of my room, I can just make out that his face is flushed and his eyes are a little glassy.

"I'm in heat," he whispers.

The relief that washes over me is immense. He is not sick. He is just in heat. My sleep addled brain finally registers the gorgeous scent that is washing over him. My body tingles all over as it responds to the pheromones he is exuding.

"Get me out of it please, before Ian notices and calls Ritchie."

I blink as I try to gather my thoughts. It's the middle of the night, Red's pheromones are overwhelming my body and even if they weren't, Red naked and in my bed would be enough to stop all my brain cells from working.

Slowly a muddled thought emerges, did he just ask me to fuck him? And he said please? As if I would be doing him a favor rather than receiving the greatest honor?

But surely Smithson will want his heat? The billionaire is hardly going to pass on the opportunity. Everyone wants an omega in heat. The experience is supposed to be legendary.

"Won't they know you are due?" I manage to say.

Red shakes his head. "My cycle is all over the place. Unpredictable."

"Stress will do that," I say, momentarily slipping into healer mode.

He stares at me, and I stare back. I don't know what time it is, but somehow I get the impression everyone else is asleep. And while we are in the middle of a vibrant city, we are very high up and the glass is thick. I can't hear a thing. It is dark and quiet in my room and it feels like Red is the only thing that exists. He is all that I see, All that I smell, The only thing I can feel. He is all that I am aware of. The only thing that I want. I don't need anything else. Just him. Only Red.

I guess my lie about being impotent was blown long ago. Even though he hasn't called me out on it. And I'm allowed to use the boys whenever I want.

If I get him out of heat quick enough, no one will ever know he was in heat. I didn't find any cameras in my room when I searched, but even if I missed them, we are under the duvet and that feels like enough privacy. There isn't really a reason not to give him what he craves. Except I'm not sure if I can.

"I...I'm not an alpha," I whisper, stating the obvious.

Some omegas need an alpha's knot to break their heat. I have no idea what Red's needs are. I don't know how his heats are normally dealt with. For all I know Ritchie could play until he has had his full and then they call an alpha in.

I want to be enough for Red, to be all that he needs and it hurts to think I might not be.

"Please. I need you inside me," says Red, ignoring my concerns.

He doesn't seem to care what I am not. His eyes are imploring. His tone pleading. I swallow dryly as every drop of blood in my body rushes to my cock. I'm suddenly very glad that I sleep naked. The thought of having to figure out how to remove pajamas seems daunting right now as well as entirely too time consuming.

I roll on top of him and he spreads his legs for me with a soft, needy whimper. The sound goes straight to my cock. Usually I like long languorous foreplay, but that is not what Red needs. He is in heat. He will be feeling desperately empty. His body will be cramping with the need to be filled. And I don't know if it's his pheromones, but my need to slide my aching cock into his soft tight flesh, is burning with an intensity I have never felt before.

I line my cock up to his hole and brush his entrance with my tip. He gives an encouraging gasp. The feel of his slick drenched hole consumes me. With a grunt, I thrust my hips and slide into him, up to the hilt in one smooth glide.

He yells, throws his head back and digs his fingers into my shoulders. A tsunami of sensation and pleasure washes over me. I'm inside Red. I'm making love to him. His ass is quivering around my hard cock. He is crying out in pleasure from my touch. Mine. I am doing this to him. I've never felt so proud in my life.

I let my hips take over. Let them take up the primal rhythm. The dance as old as time. Red rises up to meet me with every beat. Our bodies working as one. Combining to bring us both joy.

"More!" he gasps.

Since I don't have any more cock to give him, the only more I can grant him is speed and force. So I pick up both until I'm railing him into the mattress. He wails with delight and spasms as he comes. He clenches around my cock so tightly, it's like being milked, and I follow him into bliss and fall into my own orgasm.

Sparks of euphoria are dancing throughout my body. I can barely breathe. I can't see. I roll away to collapse next to him instead of on top of him.

Red whimpers, and then whines, bucking his hips up into the empty air. Still panting, I reach over and shove three fingers inside his wet hole. He relaxes and rocks gently against my fingers.

An alpha would be able to keep his cock inside Red all night. I'm going to have to do what I can while my cock recovers. Keep him full. Feed his appetite. Try to satisfy him.

I find his swollen prostate and stroke it gently. He peaks again with a soft cry but I know not to remove my fingers. Hopefully, his pheromones will affect me enough that my cock will be ready to go again soon. My mind is certainly very willing. Damn human bodies and their refractory period.

"More!" pleads Red.

"I can't give you more right now, kitten."

He lets out a very shifter sounding whine and his eyes flash amber in the dark. It should scare the shit out of me. But it sets my heart racing for an entirely different reason. Red is a beautiful, magical, powerful and supernatural being. He is a child of the moon goddess and can shift into a wolf. Stories of his kin have been woven throughout human history, both revered and feared, and here he is, allowing me the pleasure of his body. Choosing me to spend his heat with.

"More!" he demands again.

My cock is valiantly trying to stir but as well as being human, I'm not as young as I used to be. There is only one thing I can think of. I roll over to get myself into a better position. Then I carefully ease a fourth finger inside him. He moans beautifully.

"Good?" I check.

He nods eagerly.

In the dim light, I can just about make out the sight of my four fingers sinking into his body. It's an image I'm never going to forget. I'll probably be calling it up every time I wank for the rest of my life.

"Do you want more?" I ask, my voice sounding all husky and hoarse.

He nods again.

Gently I slide my fingers up and down, never all the way out, just a slight movement to open him up even more. I move my thumb to his rim to tease it. He gasps and cants his hips up in invitation.

Slowly, I add my thumb to my fingers, stretching him wide and easing my whole hand into his ass. It feels incredible. I've never fisted anyone before and I love that Red is my first.

I move my hand very carefully. He makes soft whimpers of pleasure. He feels relaxed around me. I wait a few heartbeats longer to make sure he really is ready. Then I gently curl my fingers to form a fist inside him. The noise he makes causes my cock to finally start to refill.

It's so difficult to access the thinking part of my brain to recall what I know about omega anatomy, but I just about manage it. Now I need to graze my knuckles against the spots an alpha's knot would rub.

Red's back arches and he all but howls in satisfaction. I grin. I think I've found it. I'm stretching him as wide as a knot would and if I keep hitting the right spots, it should feel as every bit as good as being knotted.

I graze the same spot again and he sings out a beautiful keening sound of pure carnal satisfaction. I do it again and he comes hard. So I do it again and again. Omegas need to come many, many times when they are in heat.

He sobs and writhes and spills. Over and over again in a gorgeous cycle. I want to watch him forever.

With one last yell, his entire body goes rigid as his lovely cock spurts weakly. Then he collapses bonelessly. Limbs all spread wide and decadent.

Carefully, I uncurl my fist and ease out of him. He gives a little murmur that sounds deeply sated. It makes me grin like the Cheshire Cat. I lay down beside him and pull him into a spoon.

He is all soft and pliant in my arms. I snuffle his hair. I've never felt happier in my life.

I have no idea if his heat has broken or if he just needs a rest. I'm delighted either way. One thing is for sure though. I'm not running away this time, and neither is he.

Red is spreading the night in my bed. Where he belongs.

Chapter Nineteen

Red

I don't know why I feel so sheepish as I creep into the kitchen. No one will know I spent the night in Brodie's room. How could they? But I have a horrible feeling that they do and it's going to be a twisted version of the walk of shame.

The sun is shining through the windows and it's just my luck that everyone apart from Blue and Gray are here eating breakfast. Everyone stops what they are doing to stare at me. Damn it. I feel my cheeks flush and that makes everything worse.

"Are you alright?" asks Ned.

The look in his eyes is savage. I'm pretty sure if I say I'm not, he'll go break Brodie's arm or something. Whatever he can get away with without risking his grandkids. It's very sweet.

"I'm fine," I say.

I'm more than fine. I'm fantastic. I'm walking on clouds and any minute now I might burst into song.

Lello squeals in delight and clasps his hands to his face. "Do you love him?"

My heart gives a strange flutter, but I laugh and shake my head. Lello pouts.

"But you like him?" he insists.

"I do," I agree and I can't stop the huge grin that takes over my face.

Lello beams at me and turns back to his breakfast. I busy myself with getting a croissant and an orange juice. I'm far too giddy to cook today. Then I sit down across from Lello and Ned.

"Tell me everything!" gushes Lello, his eyes brimming with glee.

"No, Lello, I'm not doing that."

Lello scowls at the same time as Ned mutters, "Thank heavens."

"You're so boring!" exclaims Lello but then he takes a huge bite of his toast so hopefully he is going to drop it.

I glance over at Pink and Jade. They are casting glances my way but it doesn't look like they are going to say anything. This place has made them believe that sex is something awful to be endured, and I hate that they have been robbed of something so special. They won't understand me enjoying Brodie, But I hope they won't judge me for it.

Seems I'm going to get off far lighter than I expected. That's a relief. Though I wonder how they knew. I guess some of them smelled my heat and put two and two together. I can't really blame them for gossiping, it's one of the few of life's pleasures that we get to enjoy in here. They'd never do it maliciously and I know they won't tell Ian I was in heat.

So it's all good. Maybe I will burst into that song. With a little dance routine. I haven't felt this good in forever and it's not just the afterglow of mind blowing sex. Brodie made it special. Brodie is special.

My soppy thoughts are interrupted by Blue walking in. His mask is off but Ian is right behind him and my gaze falls uneasily to the taser holstered at his hip, before returning to Blue's beaming smile and sparkling eyes. He looks much younger without the mask and that breaks my heart. Not that I'm going to show it. I don't want to ruin his good mood.

"Hey Blue!" I say as I shuffle up to make room for him.

He sits next to me and he is practically vibrating with excitement. I cast a quizzical glance at Ian, since Blue is not allowed to speak.

"He just had his first session in his soundproof room," explains Ian.

Oh, how lovely! The room Brodie arranged for him so he can sing. He really is a lovely man. And just like that, I'm back to soppy thoughts about Brodie.

Ian slides a bowl of porridge in front of Blue. "Eat and then I can put your mask back on and stop babysitting you."

Blue takes one look at it, shakes his head and points at the poached salmon that's on the counter. Ian sighs but goes and gets him some.

"Half an hour in there and you've gotten cheeky," grumbles Ian, but he doesn't sound too annoyed.

Blue tucks in happily to his fish and it's so lovely to see him looking so well. Even if Brodie isn't an agent, he is going to make our lives better. He already has. I'll forever be grateful to whatever gods brought him to us.

"Pink, once Blue here is finished, you and me are going to go to your room for some fun," says Ian.

My heart stutters, and my blood runs cold. A clang sounds as Blue drops his fork. He hastily picks it up and resumes eating. This time, super slowly. Bless him. As if delaying things ever made them better. And as if Ian is going to let him get away with that.

Pink's face has crumpled and he looks utterly miserable. Fuck Ian. What kind of sick bastard is he to want someone who clearly doesn't want him.

I should sashay over to Ian and tell him I'm ready and that I'll be much more fun. But my body is refusing to move. I'd like to think it's because I know Ian isn't in the mood for me. He wants to cause fear. He is on a power trip and needs to feel domineering. At least, I hope I've read him right, and it's not an excuse I'm telling myself so I don't feel like a coward.

Jade looks up at Ian. "Pink is still sore, take me."

Pink pushes away from the table violently, with a screech of chair leg across the floor and jumps to his feet.

"No! I'm fine."

Ian chuckles. "No need to fight over me, boys. I've got enough cock for the both of you."

I grimace. He has to know they're not fighting over him in that way. For all his flaws, I don't think he is an idiot.

"Breakfast is over, Blue," says Ian as he takes the mask out of his pocket.

So much for him waiting until Blue was finished. I guess Ian has decided he is too impatient to wait. At least Blue has eaten most of the fish and he will be allowed to eat again later. They don't starve us. And I hate that it's something I feel we need to be grateful for. This place has seriously twisted my grip on reality.

Blue obediently puts his fork down and stays motionless as Ian fixes the mask in place. Then Ian whistles at Pink like he is a dog, and the two of them leave the kitchen. Blue stares after them, wide eyed and forlorn, as if he thinks it is his fault.

I give his leg a little squeeze under the table. It's not his fault. It's not mine. It's just the harsh reality of our captivity.

Jade looks like he is going to cry. I'm so proud of him for trying to help Pink. Considering how awful Jade finds sex, it was incredibly brave of him. Unlike me. I just sat here and did absolutely nothing.

As much as I tell myself I didn't act because Ian was feeling domineering, I know a huge part of my inaction was that I selfishly didn't want to taint the memory of Brodie. I can still feel the echo of his touch upon my skin and I don't want to sully that.

I sigh. My appetite has vanished. Along with my good mood.

I really hope Brodie is here to save us. And I pray he does it soon.

Chapter Twenty

Brodie

Red has saved me so much time by showing me the server room. I would have found it, eventually. But I can't just go around blatantly nosing around. Slow and steady while raising absolutely no suspicion is the only way that works. It's my tried and tested method and why I am good at what I do.

Which begs the question, why the hell am I in the server room now? It's far too soon. I'm rushing things because I have allowed my emotions to get the better of me. I want to get the boys out of here as soon as possible. I want Red to be free. And that desire has driven me to take risks that I would never normally contemplate.

It's stupid. Part of me knows it. Messing up will not get the boys out of here quicker, it's going to get me caught and dead. And then security, background checks and vetting is going to be tightened up and it will take the Council forever to get someone else in here. Meaning my stupidity is only going to prolong the boys' captivity, not shorten it.

I need to come to my senses and get out of here before I get caught. Just as that thought crosses my mind, my device beeps softly, indicating that it has finished downloading. It really is time to leave. I hope I've found something about the security plans, both practical and magical. Anything that will enable me to get the boys out of here. But I know it's not as simple as that. Smithson needs to be shut down completely. There is little point in leaving him free to build up a replacement harem.

Deep breath. That's not my riddle to solve. My part is to acquire the information. Greater minds than mine will puzzle out what to do with it.

Right now, I need to focus on getting back to my room without being seen. Adrenaline surges through me as suddenly the distance seems impossibly far. Just breathe. I can do this.

Cautiously, I head out. It feels like I've only gone a few steps when, from above my head, I hear the whir of a camera shifting position. Fuck. I thought they were on five minute movements. Did I trigger something? Did I calculate it wrong? Whichever it is, I'm screwed. I've just been filmed walking away from a part of the penthouse I have no business being in.

My heart is racing and there is only one thing I can think of. It's going to break me but consequences are for later. I put a glower on my face and start to stomp around. Red isn't in the party area. I try the roof terrace next and he is not there either. This is great. If he is actually hard to find, it's all the more believable. I can make people think that the only reason I was by the servers was because I was looking for Red.

I pass Lello in the hallway. "Where is Red?" I snap. I really hope he isn't in his room. It would seem strange if I was stomping around every corner of the penthouse looking for him, if he was just in his room the whole time.

"In Pink's room," answers Lello with an uneasy look in his big blue eyes.

I storm past him to Pink's room and fling the door open with far more force than is necessary. Red, Pink and Jade are sitting on the bed playing cards. They all flinch at my abrupt arrival and then stare at me warily.

"Why the fuck do you think you can hide from me, Red?" I growl.

Red put's his cards down as his gaze tracks over my face. Trying to read me. Trying to figure out what is going on. The faint look of hurt confusion in his beautiful eyes is too much to bear.

I stride up to him and grab his arm. "You were supposed to be in my room twenty minutes ago," I snarl.

The hope that flashes across his face, feels like a punch in the gut. He wants to believe that I'm up to something. He really does, but there is a lot of doubt in his expression. I can't blame him for that. He has been surrounded by bastards for so long and he has no real reason to believe that I'm not one. It still hurts though.

"I...I forgot," he stammers.

Is he playing along, or is he just trying to appease me? Fuck. I wish I knew. He damn well knows I didn't ask him to be anywhere, but that doesn't mean I don't have a dollop of crazy along with my bastard.

I haul him out of Pink's room and nearly run into Ian in the hallway. Just as I was expecting. He has come to investigate what I am doing. The overseer raises an eyebrow.

"Red, giving you trouble?"

"Nothing I can't handle," I growl.

Ian chuckles. "Fair enough, just remember not to leave a mark or make him unable to work. Do you want a taser?"

The overseer tilts his head at me and smirks. Shit, I think I let my horrified expression show. This is a disaster.

"I know they seem very human, but they aren't. They are just animals. Animals that are good for fucking. Don't forget that."

I open and close my mouth a few times before words come out. "Pink is human."

"Not really, not with all his magic shit. He is nothing more than a freak."

I stare at Ian for a long moment while I battle to keep a blank expression. I shouldn't be so shocked by what he is saying, but it has rattled me. I hadn't realized just how vile he is and I'm normally a good judge of character.

"You're right. They are pretty enough that sometimes I forget," I hear myself say.

Thank heavens some small part of my brain is still functioning and able to carry out my job. What the hell is wrong with me? I used to be good at this. This absolutely has to be my last mission. I've clearly finally cracked. They say it happens to all agents eventually. I was just too arrogant to believe it would ever happen to me.

Ian chuckles again, and I nod at him before dragging Red down the hallway to my room. As soon as we get inside, I slam the door shut.

"What is..." starts Red but I can't let him continue.

Ian was suspicious, I know he was. I don't think there are any cameras in my room, but nothing is certain, and there might be bugs. And I just can't take any more risks right now. None at all.

If Ian was tracking my movements, I've already fucked up. I've done something to arouse his curiosity and his need to keep an eye on me. I didn't find any cameras in my room last time I looked. That doesn't mean there is none in here now.

I throw Red against the wall and kiss him. Kiss him deeply and savagely. Desperately. Can I tell him with this kiss not to say anything? Can I say I'm sorry? Can I beg him to trust me and go along with whatever I do?

The safest thing for Red is if he knows nothing, if he thinks I'm just another captor. But I think that ship has well and truly sailed. If truth be told, I think it left the moment I caught him in my arms and stared into his eyes. He saw right through me the moment our gazes locked. Red has always known that something was up. He just needs to keep pretending that he doesn't.

And I'm going to have to punish him for something he hasn't done, for the sake of us all.

Chapter
Twenty-One

Brodie

R eluctantly I break away from the kiss. Red stares up at me, breathless and with swollen lips. Fuck. He is so gorgeous I could drown in his beautiful eyes forever. I can't believe he even notices me. Talk about being out of my league. And now I'm going to destroy everything.

"You shouldn't have disobeyed me," I say.

His eyes flash with something, and he nods. I think he understands. Oh gods! I pray with every fiber of my being that he understands.

Slowly and with every ounce of menace that I can muster, I pull off my belt. It slides through my belt hoops with a soft swooshing sound. Red's eyes widen and he swallows. Shit. I thought spanking might be fun. There is no way on earth I can make myself just beat him. At least this way there might be some pleasure with the pain. But he looks scared.

My guts are churning and I think I might be sick. I want to hold him in my arms and pepper him with gentle kisses until everything bad goes away.

"Bend over the bed," I order.

Gracefully, he moves past me and obeys my command. The red silk trousers do nothing to hide the glorious shape of his ass. My treacherous cock stirs with interest. I am a monster.

There might not be any cameras. There might not be any bugs. We could be alone and in full privacy. I could be hurting him for no reason at all. On the other hand, if Ian is watching, I need to make this look good. I need to quash any suspicions.

My throat is so tight I can't swallow. My hands curl the belt into a loop. I don't want to hit Red with it, not if he is going to hate it. And I can well imagine that he will. He has probably been beaten so much that pain will never be kinky for him. It will always just be pain.

But there is nothing I can do about that. I have to hit him. Hit him and hope he can forgive me. I take a deep breath. Red is holding very still for me, and I wish I knew what was going through his head.

I flick back my wrist and strike. The belt makes an awful noise and Red flinches, but doesn't make a noise. I don't think I have the skill to make this look worse than it is, but I'm going to try my best. I'm going to try to hit him in a way that looks impressive but doesn't hurt too much. It's the best I can do.

I hit him again. The belt thwacks against his ass cheeks and the faint jiggle they give excites my cock. His ass is far too firm to give a proper bounce but the darker part of me still likes what it sees.

My stomach heaves with guilt. If I get a kick out of this, it confirms that I am a dark twisted bastard. The only thing left to question is if it is the years of shady work that have twisted me or was I born this way? But I guess that is a moot point. Neither option redeems me. Red is not going to care why I am enjoying hurting him.

I lash out with the belt again. Red still doesn't make a sound. He is so strong. So brave. I don't think I've ever admired anyone more.

Hitting him again feels awful, but my muscles are getting the idea and they pick up a rhythm that allows my mind to switch off. I'm not allowed to leave marks on him or hurt him so much that he is unable to work. That's one saving grace. A perfect excuse not to go too far.

The belt cracks through the air once again before hitting Red's ass, this time a pained hiss escapes him. The noise tears into my soul and claws at my heart. Fuck this. I fling the belt away from me in disgust. Then I stride up to Red and haul him up from the bed and then down onto his knees.

Holding him in place with one hand on his shoulder, I free my cock with my other hand. Red obediently opens his mouth without me saying anything. I close my eyes and shove my cock into his mouth, deep enough to make him gag.

I move one hand to his luxurious hair and grab a fist full. I move my other hand to his throat. Then I fuck his face, hard.

The soft, wet heat of his mouth and throat feels amazing. A deep groan escapes me. The harder and faster I fuck him, the sooner I will come and this will all be over. And face fucking and choking always looks and sounds brutal.

Red has gone lax in my grip. He is pliantly letting me use him. I thrust deep and hold still. I know he can't breathe, but he doesn't try to fight me. I tighten my fingers around his throat and imagine that I can feel my cock in there. He feels so damn good.

I start thrusting again. I'm assuming he is experienced enough to time getting enough air into his lungs around my cock. I don't want to make him pass out.

A memory plays in my mind of the first time Red was on his knees before me. He had tensed when I had run my hands through his hair and then seemed so delighted when I didn't take control. Now here I am, using him like a blow-up doll. Making him gag repeatedly.

My balls start to draw up. My body has no shame, no conscience. It only knows that my cock is bathed in wet soft heat and receiving delicious friction. I grunt as I come. My seed spills down Red's throat in what feels like a mechanical release. It feels nothing like the previous orgasms I have had with him. There is no joy in this.

I shove him away from me roughly and he falls back onto his ass, leaning against the bed. He is gasping for air and his face is covered in tears and snot. He looks wrecked, ruined. And still the most beautiful boy I have ever seen.

I want to pull him into my arms, carry him to the bed and cuddle him. Praise him. Tell him how well he did. Tell him I'm sorry. But that would undo everything I just did.

It would make his suffering and my cruelty be for nothing. The one silver lining in this awful cloud is if Ian was watching, he will now be assured that I'm just another slimeball bastard like him. My cover is safe. The mission is still on. I can continue to work on getting Red and the whole Rainbow out of here.

That is what really matters. Not Red hating me. In the grand scheme of things, that doesn't matter at all.

My heart clenches painfully. I rub at my chest as if it is merely a physical pain. If only it were. Those are far easier to deal with and far simpler to fix.

"Get out," I rasp.

Red scrambles to his feet and flees, while still gasping for air. He keeps his head down and doesn't look at me at all. I have no idea what he is thinking. Does he understand that it was all a ruse to cover up my mistake?

I run my hands through my hair. Fuck. He is never going to forgive me, is he? Even if he understands my reasons, the fact is, he paid for my fuck up. There is nothing fair about that at all.

Despondently, I flop onto the bed. I don't feel like ever getting up. I just want to lie here forever and try to pretend that the world does not exist.

But now that it's still and quiet, I can feel the device in my pocket. It's almost as if I can feel the weight of its secrets. Ones that might just be the key to the boys' freedom. I need to get up and start unraveling them.

As my mom always said, there is no rest for the wicked.

Chapter Twenty-Two

Red

I stagger down the hallway towards my room. When I look up and see Ned leaning on my door with his arms crossed, I'm not surprised.

"Not now Ned," I mutter as I barge past him.

I'm keeping my head down so he doesn't see the state I'm in, but I have a sinking feeling that he can just tell. I head straight for my bathroom and start frantically washing my face. The cool water feels good. Soothing. It's clearing my mind and calming my thoughts.

I don't grab a towel, I just lean over the sink with my hands braced on either side and let the water drip off of me. My ass feels like it's on fire. But it's my heart that really hurts.

I've received worse treatment. Much worse. Physically this is nothing, it should be like water off a duck's back. But I've never received it from someone I liked before. Someone I had feelings for. Someone I trusted.

I take in a deep shuddering breath. He had to have his reasons, I'm sure of it. I saw the conflict in his eyes when he burst into Pink's room. I felt the apology in his savage kiss. Or am I just seeing what I want to see? Pathetically clinging onto tiny scraps of hope and building up a picture that isn't there?

My stomach churns painfully. No, I can't believe that. I don't want to believe that. Brodie never told me to go to his room today. And while it's agony to think he might just be another sadistic bastard, I just can't believe he is deranged. Everything in me balks at that idea, which then makes me feel awful that I can believe he is a violent asshole.

"Red?" calls Ned through my bathroom door.

"I'm fine!"

"Come out then!" he insists.

Sometimes friends are so annoying. I stomp over to the door, fling it open and stare at Ned right in the eye.

"See? I'm fine!"

Ned huffs and looks entirely unconvinced. Is he going to do something to Brodie? Part of me is horrified at the thought, another part is fucking gleeful. Hells, I'm definitely a confused mess right now.

Suddenly, Lello bounds in and into my arms. The force of his hug knocks me back a step but wrapping my arms around him and feeling the warm weight of him is comforting.

"I'm sorry I told him where you were," Lello whispers softly.

"Hey," I say. "It's fine, he would have found me eventually and just been even more angry."

Lello looks up at me with his big blue eyes. "I did the right thing?"

"You sure did," I say with a smile.

My gaze meets Ned and the vampire is scowling. He probably doesn't approve that I'm comforting Lello, instead of being comforted myself, but he knows what the kelpie is like. Lello is a sweet innocent who needs all the love. Besides, I like the distraction and being the caregiver is a role I'm happy in. Unlike being the receiver.

"Cuddle time!" declares Lello and suddenly I'm being towed towards my bed.

I end up lying on it as the little spoon as Lello curls around my back with his arms around my waist.

"You too, Ned!" demands Lello.

Ned sighs but climbs into the bed and lies down in front of me. He drapes his arm over me and I feel like a sandwich. It's lovely though. It reminds me of being a pup and sleeping in a big puppy pile with the other kids in my pack.

A sudden wave of homesickness washes over me. Would being claimed by an alpha really have been so bad? I might have been chosen by a nice one. I could have ended up with a happy pack. My alpha could have chosen a surrogate and I could have pups by now. And even if I had been claimed by an alphahole, it would just be one douchebag to deal with. One douchebag to give my body to.

"I feel like such a molly," mutters Ned.

"What's a molly?" asks Lello from behind me.

"It's a really old word for a gay man," I say.

Ned's eyes narrow. "Make me feel ancient, why don't you?"

"You are old!" giggles Lello. "And gay. And you do like cuddles so stop pretending that you don't."

The vampire makes a grumpy face but I can see a fond smile in his eyes, trying to get out. It makes me wonder if he was always cantankerous. Pondering that seems like a great distraction and right now I'd rather think about anything else other than Brodie.

So I try to imagine Ned as he was before. And suddenly I can see him as a young cheerful human, in what? 1930s or 1940s? A gorgeous gay man with his whole human life ahead of him. I've never asked but I've always had the impression that he never wanted to be turned and that it was done against his will.

As young as he was when he died, I know he was married with a baby and that he loved his wife, who was a lesbian. The times they were in forced them into a marriage, to protect them both, but it worked well for them and they were happy.

Then he was stolen from that life. Given his stunning good looks, I'm not surprised he caught a vampire's eye. And now Ritchie has stolen him from his second life. All because I let Ritchie know about paranormals and set him down the path of hunting for a collection.

I'm such a selfish pig-headed idiot. If I had just stayed in my pack, none of this would ever have happened. Ned, Lello and all the others would be free. All this suffering and misery because I thought I was too good to be mated.

To my horror, tears start to well. Hastily I try to blink them away, but it's too late, Ned has seen them. His face fills with pity, which just sets me off even more. I sob and Lello snuggles even closer and tightens his grip on me.

"Oh hells!" exclaims Ned. "Don't cry about Brodie!"

I'm not crying about Brodie. I don't think? Actually, maybe I am. As much as I was trying desperately not to think about him. Maybe I'm crying about everything that is awful in my life.

Everything that hurts is all piled together in a giant mountain of pain and I've just been struck by an avalanche.

"I'm far too fucking soft," mutters Ned. "Lello, cover your ears."

Lello's arm disappears from around my waist and the kelpie starts singing "La, la, la," very loudly.

"Don't tell a soul what I'm about to tell you, it's a vampire secret."

That's enough to distract me from crying. I sniffle and nod my agreement.

Ned takes a deep breath, even though I'm sure he doesn't need to breathe at all. I guess some habits don't die easily.

"I drank his blood. It means I know things. Trust him."

I stare deep into Ned's brown eyes. The vampire is deadly serious. Not that he would joke about something like this. The connotations of his words spin around in my mind. Brodie is a good person. Brodie had his reasons and he didn't want to hurt me.

Ned reaches over me to tap Lello. The annoying la-la's stop and Lello's arm snakes back around me.

My thoughts echo and repeat. Brodie is a good person. I didn't imagine the connection between us. He is special, just like I thought. The hope that reignites in my heart hurts. It burns away my feelings of devastation and loss and suddenly I'm crying harder than before.

"Ned! What did you say to Red!" admonishes Lello crossly.

"They are happy tears," explains Ned wearily.

"Oh! That's good then," says Lello.

Yes, it is. It's very, very good. Everything is going to be fine. My sudden faith in that, and Brodie, is absolute. It just might be a bumpy road to get there.

But what's a few more bumps?

Chapter Twenty-Three

Brodie

S weat is dripping into my eyes. My lungs are screaming and my leg muscles are in agony but I still haven't been able to run away from my hurt. I haven't reached a place where I can forget what I did to Red. Maybe I never will. I certainly don't deserve too. I should just run on this treadmill forever like some sort of modern day Sisyphus.

"Brodie?" someone says.

I hit the stop switch, grab my towel and wipe the sweat from my eyes so I can see who I'm talking to. I look over and see it is Pink hovering in the gym's doorway.

"Sorry to bother you," he begins but I interrupt him by walking over.

"It's fine, shall we go to the med room?" I'm still breathing heavily but he doesn't seem to mind.

He nods and we walk together in silence. I know Ian used him recently but I already checked on him after that and he said he was fine. Did he lie? Or is something else wrong?

We reach the med room and Pink hops up onto the examination table. I close the door and patiently wait for him to say what he needs.

"I'm ripe," he says while looking at the floor.

Okay, so he is full of magic and needs to have sex with a magic wielder to empty him. It is a regular occurrence for him, similar to Red going into heat. It shouldn't be a problem. Not medically anyway.

"I was wondering if there was a way to stop it?" he asks.

Oh shit, I'm such an idiot. Yeah being ripe when you are not a sex slave, isn't a problem. When you are one, it must be awful. Your own body betraying you with its lust and need for whatever scumbag is bending you over. Poor kid. I'm thrilled he trusts me enough to ask and I hate to let him down, but there really is nothing I can do.

"I'm afraid not," I say as gently as I can.

He sighs as if it's exactly what he was expecting to hear. Then he lifts his head and stares at me intently with his big brown eyes.

"Could you..."

My throat goes dry and I think I'm blushing. I'm flattered, but he is just a kid and I couldn't. Not even as a kindness. Nevermind that my first reaction is to think of it as a betrayal to Red.

My second thought is dismay. Surely he knows how I treated Red, and he still thinks of me as the better option? That says everything I need to know about the bastards he is used to dealing with.

"It wouldn't work," I say hoarsely. "Some healers do have a fair amount of healing magic, but I don't. I have very little. I heal more like a modern doctor than by magic. I can't empty you."

Pink holds my gaze for a moment longer, then he looks at the floor again. "Okay," he says tonelessly.

"Who normally does it?" I ask.

"Lord Hyde. He is a mage. He comes in and sets the perimeter wards in exchange."

My heart thuds. This is fantastic information. Now I know who is protecting the penthouse so iron tight with magic that no one can get in without permission.

"Will Ian call him?" I ask.

Pink nods. "Yeah, I'll go tell him I'm ripe."

"Will he call Ritchie first?"

Pink gives a little weary sigh, "Yeah."

I knew Ritchie would want a desperate, frantic Pink in his bed. I suspect it's the main reason the vessel is part of his collection, aside from his stunning good looks. But the confirmation still makes my guts twist.

"I think Ritchie is in China," I say calmly.

I really shouldn't divulge that I know this. There is no reason for me to have this information, except for my snooping, but I need to give the boy some hope. Being taken by just this Lord Hyde has got to be better than being tormented by Ritchie first and then the mage.

Pink looks at me, and I see a little flash of something in his sad eyes. "But I still need Lord Hyde."

I nod in agreement, there really isn't anything to say to that.

He slides off the table and walks away sadly with a defeated drop to his shoulders. The sight breaks my heart. I wish with all my soul there was something I could do. But there is nothing. Nothing except stalking this mage when he arrives and trying to spy on him as he sets the wards. If I can see the configuration he uses, that information will help another mage to dismantle them. And if the Council can swoop in here and free all the boys. Pink's suffering, all the boys' suffering will be over.

I just have to make sure I'm not caught.

I catch a glimpse of Lord Hyde as he strolls into the penthouse accompanied by Ian. He is a middle-aged man dressed in an impeccably tailored suit that just screams money. I duck back into my room before he sees me. Then I pace around for fifteen long minutes, as I desperately try not to think about what is happening in Pink's room.

Then I start lurking in the vicinity of Pink's door. I'm going to casually mention to Ian later how I was desperately excited to meet a lord and wanted to talk to him to ask about investment tips.

Hopefully, if he is watching me on camera, that will quell any suspicions about my strange behavior.

Eventually, Hyde comes out of Pink's room. Finally! Carefully I hide my relief and stride up to the mage.

"Does he need me?" I say with a cocky smile as I gesture at Pink's door. "I'm the healer."

Hyde looks at me as if I am a piece of shit on his shoe. "No. He knows his place."

I grin as my stomach heaves in disgust. "Glad to hear it!"

The mage sneers at me, clearly fully expecting me to fuck off. But he is not going to be so lucky.

"I was wondering if you had any investment tips? You look like a man who knows his business."

Hyde raises one disapproving eyebrow. "Why would I give advice for free?"

Taking a leaf out of Ian's book, I slap Hyde on the back and it's deeply satisfying. Maybe I'll take it up and start doing it to everyone.

"Good point!" I exclaim happily. "How about I give you a cut? Say ten per cent?"

"How much are you looking to invest?" Hyde asks suspiciously, but as I hoped, there is a gleam of avarice in his eyes. Rich people always want more.

Now I just need to think of an amount that is tempting for him, yet believable. I don't look like I have money or come from money. But I'm not going to let that stop me.

"One million," I say proudly as I puff up my chest.

Hyde's deeply skeptical look is almost comical.

"Granny left me her house. Old bird was born and bred in Hackney. Lived there her whole life. Bought a 3 bed semi in the 50s for small change and I just got a cool one point five mill for it."

Hyde looks me up and down while I beam like an idiot. Hackney was a shitty part of London when I was a kid but now it's ridiculously trendy. With London already having crazy house prices, a three-bed semi in Hackney would easily go for two to two and a half million. I'm making myself out to be an easily played idiot and I can tell he is tempted.

"But hey, I don't want to keep you. Why don't we chat while you work?" I say with my best affable smile.

The mage scrutinizes me for a moment longer and then he nods decisively before turning to lead the way. I feel like doing a fist bump of joy but I manage to restrain myself. This is all working perfectly. He is arrogant enough to believe that I won't have a clue what I'm looking at, so I'm going to be able to see exactly what he does.

Hopefully, having that in my report is going to make the Grand Master slightly less pissed off at having to scramble to make a paper trail and put a million in my bank account so that my story checks out. Because I just know Hyde is going to look into it. He is definitely the type.

But I don't care. I don't care if the entire world hates me. I'm getting these boys out of here if it's the last thing I do.

Chapter
Twenty-Four

Red

It's tricky keeping an eye on the door behind me while I'm getting everything ready in the kitchen, but I manage it and it soon pays off.

Brodie walks in, sees me and turns to scarper.

"Hey!" I call, stopping him in his tracks.

He turns around so slowly it's almost comical. When he finally makes it, his eyes are wide and I think he is a little sweaty. It makes my heart feel all fluttery. Any tiny lingering doubts I had are obliterated by his reactions. A sadistic bastard would not have shame and guilt etched into every line of their body.

"Are you as good at chopping veg as you are at flipping pancakes?" I ask with a smile. "I'm making a Sunday roast and could do with a hand."

Brodie blinks slowly as he tries to process what is going on. I feel sorry for him, I really do. Acting like nothing happened isn't the best course of action but it is the only one I can think of. I can't exactly say out loud, 'I strongly suspect you are an agent and you beat me and choked me for a reason and my vampire friend told me to trust you, so I do and I forgive you.'

The only thing I can do is make clear that I do forgive him and that there are no hard feelings. I don't think Ian will find it suspicious, we are all used to being treated like crap. It's just another day.

I hold out a knife to him, handle first. His gaze drops to it and he licks his lips. He is trembling ever so slightly, as if he thinks I'm about to flip it over and plunge it into his heart.

Cautiously he steps forward and reaches for it, our fingers brush and he freezes. His gaze locks with mine. I wonder if he felt that jolt of electricity too? I stare deep into his eyes and try to convey everything I want to say to him. He stares back at me and time slows to a stop. The rest of the universe falls away. There is only us.

After an eternity, he licks his lips again and nods. He takes the knife from my hand and the spell is broken. I blink. Did he understand me?

I hate this. I wish we could talk. But there are cameras and sound recorders nearly everywhere in the penthouse. We have to act as if every movement and every word is being observed. Asking him to get me out of heat had been risky enough, but the punishment wouldn't have been too bad. Brodie would have been fired at worst.

Talks about being an agent would get us killed. It's simply not worth the risk. As much as it pains me. There is nothing I can do about it.

I'd love to know what he is thinking and feeling. Does he like me? Is this connection I feel between us, all in my head?

Ugh. On second thoughts maybe it is good that we can't talk. It means I can't have all my hopes and dreams dashed and I can keep skipping along in my happy little fantasy that Brodie likes me.

"What do you want chopped first?" he asks.

"Potatoes."

"In quarters, for roasting?"

"Yep," I nod.

"Do you want them peeled?"

I gasp. "Hell no! The skins are the best bit!"

He grins, "Man after my own heart."

That makes my heart flutter like crazy. I grin back at him and then get to work greasing a pan. We work in companionable silence for a while. It feels nice, this simple domesticity. One day I hope this will be my life. A little home with Brodie somewhere. I could cook dinner every night and he could rail me until I scream.

"Are you okay?" asks Brodie gently.

I flinch and for one wild moment I think he has read my mind and is questioning my sanity.

"Ah… yeah, I'm great," I say.

He pauses and stares at me for a moment before resuming his chopping. Now I feel myself flushing. Damn my dirty mind. Now Brodie thinks I'm acting strange, which is going to worry him. And I'm not brave enough to confess.

"This is a lot of veg," he remarks, and I'm grateful for the change of subject.

I glance over the pile. Is it? It looks like a normal amount to me. I look at him in alarm. I haven't misjudged, have I?

He gives me a wry smile. "It was just my mom and me growing up and now I live alone. Cooking for me is nothing like preparing food for a pack."

Wow. I can't even imagine cooking for just one or two people. That must be strange. In my brief period of freedom, when I was working as a dancer, I never stayed anywhere with a kitchen. I existed on a diet of snacks and takeaway.

I'm going to have to adjust my little daydream of living with Brodie. In my mental image, I was chopping a mountain of carrots. There is going to be a lot to learn about a human family way of living. Unless Brodie is happy to live in a non-human way and is happy for all the boys to live with us. My hands freeze for a moment as I realize what I am doing. I'm not just daydreaming, I'm assuming. I'm assuming that Brodie is going to get us out of here and then take me to live with him.

I'm losing my mind.

"You live alone? No boyfriend? Girlfriend?" I ask while attempting a casual tone.

He shakes his head, "Never met anyone special."

There are plenty of potatoes in his reach, but he stretches over to grab one that has rolled away to my side of the counter. It puts his body very close to mine, intimately so, and I sneak in a big gulp of his lovely scent.

"Until now," he whispers softly.

He straightens up with his reclaimed potato and stares at me. I stare back and feel my eyes watering. He smiles softly and I smile back. My heart is thumping like crazy. The most romantic moment of my life involves potatoes and I don't even care.

He goes back to chopping, so I go back to greasing and try to pretend nothing just happened. Like he didn't just up end my entire universe and make everything worthwhile.

Now I really want to escape Ritchie. There is a future waiting for me. One with Brodie in it.

My mind darts whirring with determination. I need to puzzle out every single way I can help Brodie and I need to do it as soon as possible.

I'm getting out of here if it is the last thing I do.

Chapter Twenty-Five

Brodie

I hear laughter coming from the kitchen as I pass by, so I pop my head in. All the boys, apart from Gray, are sitting around a table playing monopoly. It's lovely to see them enjoying themselves and to see Blue out of his pool. Being allowed to sing is really helping him and I'm glad I was able to make that improvement. I've made someone's life better in one small way at least.

I leave them to it and continue my journey to the roof terrace. My thoughts turn to the one missing boy. Gray is still trapped, chained to his bed. I've since discovered that moment of lucidity I saw was rare. He is not really with it most of the time. He hardly even opens his eyes. But the boys still make sure to take turns going into his room and chat nonsense at him so he is not alone all of the time.

I'm not sure if my attempts at physiotherapy are helping, but they are the best I can do. It's going to be a long hard journey before he is well enough to join the others for monopoly.

I stop my thoughts with a huff. That's never going to happen, because I'm getting them all out of here soon. He doesn't need to get well enough to join them, because they are all going to be free. Well, Gray will be as free as a dangerous demon can be allowed to be.

A weary sigh escapes me. It's not my problem to fix. I just need to get all the information I can to the Council. They will take it from there.

A blast of chilly air hits me as I open the door to the roof terrace. It's a gray overcast day in London. It's supposed to be early summer but as usual the British weather is paying no heed to that.

I walk over to the glass wall that encircles the terrace. The view really is fantastic. I take the joint out of my pocket and light it up. It's hard not to cough against the bitter smoke but I persevere. I need an excuse to be lingering out here. Hopefully, it won't take too long for the small data device in my pocket to pick up the encrypted signal and transmit all its info. I just need to stand here while it works.

The smoke burns my lungs as I lean on the railing and take in the view. I let my mind wander and I purposefully relax all my muscles so that my body language looks nonchalant. If anyone is watching me, they will think I'm perfectly at ease and just enjoying a joint. When actually I'm a ball of tension and anxiety. I'm worried if the device will work, or if I've found enough information. I'm also floundering in feelings about Red. How can he forgive me so easily? And I swear he knows why I'm really here, and if he has figured it out, who else has?

Do I need to convince Red that he is wrong? Am I even strong enough to do that? On and on my turbulent thoughts whirl with no end or peace in sight.

It feels like it takes forever to work my way through the joint but finally it has burned down to the roach and that means the device should have had enough time to work and I can go back inside now.

The door slams behind me, making me jump. It's Red. He rushes over to me, looking very flustered. I don't have a good feeling about this.

"A guest has arrived and chosen Blue!"

Oh shit! I think lights in Blue's pool flicker when there is a guest arriving, but I'd been looking at the view and hadn't seen the announcement. I quickly flick the remnants of my joint onto the floor and hurry back inside with Red. This isn't good at all.

By the time we arrive, Blue is already in his room with the guest. Everyone is standing around the closed door. Even Ian.

There is nothing I can do. Nothing. Just stand here idly, letting it happen and then run in and deal with the aftermath. I'm going to be sick. Red's hand slips into mine and I give him a grateful squeeze. I'm not sure who is comforting who but I guess that doesn't matter. Comforting each other works just as well.

There is no sound at all coming from Blue's room, which has to be a good sign. Except, oh fuck. The mask. He could be screaming right now and no one would hear him. My stomach heaves and a strange ringing noise starts in my ear. Red's grip on my hand tightens, it's definitely him comforting me now and I shouldn't feel ashamed of that. Toxic masculinity is bullshit.

I glance over at Ian. His attention is fixed on the screen of the tablet he is holding. It's the camera feed from Blue's room,

I suddenly realize. The overseer looks up at me. He looks upset and worried. Is he going to do something to stop this?

"Dude isn't doing anything he's not allowed to," he says, answering my unasked question.

His gaze drops back to the tablet.

"Blue?" I ask tentatively. Maybe he is doing okay. Maybe the idea is terrifying but actually getting on with it is bearable.

Ian shakes his head sadly. I step towards him before I realize what I am doing. His head snaps up and he backs away from me.

"Nah man, trust me. You don't want to see this. I don't want to see this, but someone has to keep an eye on things."

I stare at the overseer. His behavior is really confusing me. I had written him off as a heartless bastard. He has no qualms about taking Pink without his consent. So why the sudden concern?

"I thought the boys were nothing but pretty animals?" I growl, sounding far more confrontational than I should. Red's grip on me tightens enough to cut off my circulation. Fuck he is strong.

Ian doesn't seem angered by my tone, he merely raises an eyebrow. "I don't kick normal puppies either."

I turn away from him before I unleash all of my rage on him. Beating him to death will solve nothing, it will only make everything worse. I need to keep my shit together.

Breathe. Just breathe. Concentrate on that. In and out. It feels like I've been standing here breathing for a millennium. When suddenly I hear movement from inside Blue's room.

The door swings open and an enormous man strolls out with a shit-eating grin on his face. Recognition sparks through me like a slap in the face. I've seen him in the media. He is a famous pro wrestler. My sympathy for Blue increases tenfold. This man is huge, and Blue, like all the boys, is a slender little thing. The size difference alone would make it traumatic.

Ian steps forward to walk him out and I shake my head to clear it, before dashing into Blue's room with all the other boys.

Blue is naked and curled up in a ball in the corner of his room. He is trembling and his shoulders are heaving. Red runs up to him and I watch in horror as Blue flinches away and tries to climb up the wall. I have a horrible feeling that he is shrieking in terror underneath his mask.

Red places a hand on his shoulder, and suddenly Ned is there too but Blue lashes out frantically. He is hysterical. And only getting more and more worked up by the minute.

I run to the med room and grab my bag. When I get back, Blue is even worse. It's taking Red, Ned and Lello to hold him. It's the right thing to do. Blue is panicking and could easily hurt himself or someone else. Sirens are as deadly as they are beautiful.

I have no choice, But I still hate it. Hastily, I pull the necessary equipment out of my bag, calculating the correct dose in my head. It takes mere seconds to draw up a syringe full of sedative but it feels like it takes far too long.

"Hold him still," I say as I approach.

The three of them do and I quickly jab the needle into Blue's arm. He stills and slumps almost immediately. I safely dispose of the needle and turn back to Blue's slumped form.

"Let's get him on the bed," I say.

Three paranormals don't need any help to carry one siren, so I just watch. I think about Red's little bed in his closet and I feel awful for returning Blue to the scene of his trauma but I can't examine him in a closet.

"Everyone out apart from Red," I order.

Obediently the room empties, and the door shuts. The sudden stillness feels strange. Red stares at me, his eyes wide and solemn.

"I need to examine him," I say.

Red nods and moves decisively to the bed. He efficiently and gently spreads Blue's legs. I swallow, quickly glove up and carry out my examination as swiftly as possible. Thankfully, he is only swollen and tender down there. Quickly I check over the rest of him for any bruises, but his pale, slightly glimmering skin is unmarked. His assaulter didn't hurt him physically.

I nod at Red and he quickly moves Blue into a more dignified position and then pulls the duvet over to cover him. I dispose of my gloves and open Blue's door. Sure enough, all the boys are right outside, practically leaning on the wood. I step aside and let them in.

They all swarm over and onto the bed. Making Blue the center of a giant puppy pile. The sight eases my aching heart. Blue has been through hell, but he has people who love him.

I turn to go but Red stops me with a gesture. He pats the space on the edge of the bed next to him and I smile softly. No one seems to object as I make my way over. Have I really been accepted so easily? Despite the way I treated Red?

I carefully crawl onto the bed and wriggle into position until I am spooning Red as he cuddles Blue. This is nice. I can feel the tension in my muscles draining away. Touch is so soothing, healing, strengthening. It's exactly what Blue needs. Okay, it's what I need too. And this way I can also keep a close eye on him.

I really hope he is feeling calmer when he comes round and that I won't have to sedate him again. And I really fucking hope my files uploaded and got through to the Council. This all needs to end and it needs to end soon.

Or I'm going to take matters into my own hands.

Chapter Twenty-Six

Red

It's nearly time to go meet Brodie on the roof terrace. So I need to finish getting ready. I know joining him to help keep an eye on Blue is not a date, but it's the closest thing to one I'm ever going to get. Therefore, I'm making the most of it. A boy has got to dream.

Which is making getting ready a bit difficult. The trick I'm going for is to put on enough makeup to look good, without looking like I'm treating this as a date, or being frivolous. Because it really isn't a frivolous situation.

Blue is still very traumatized. He is hiding in the bottom of his pool and not coming out for anything. Lello had to swim down to him and report back to Brodie. So I don't want to give the impression that I think joining Brodie for a shift by Blue's pool is a lighthearted matter.

But I still want to look good for Brodie. I sigh. Maybe I am vain. Vain and shallow and selfish. Blue is suffering and I want to look pretty. I drop the makeup brush. Shall I scrub off what I have put on? I stare at myself in the mirror. No, I think it's fine. It's very subtle. I just won't put on anymore.

At least I don't have to stress about what to wear. I even wear these stupid clothes in my dreams now. If I ever get out of here, I'm never wearing the color red again for as long as I live.

The AI assistant beeps softly to tell me the timer I set is up. Time to go. A whole swarm of butterflies takes over my stomach. Okay, I need to take a deep breath and stop being silly.

I walk through the penthouse at super speed, as if I'm desperate to see Brodie. I really am acting like a teenager with their first crush, but then again, I think Brodie is my first crush. I've never felt this way about anyone. Even in the height of being dazzled and excited by Ritchie, I never felt like this.

The blast of night-time city air that hits me as I open the door, overwhelms me for a moment. So many scents all tangled together. It takes me a moment to calm my senses. Then I see Brodie. He has laid out a blanket and surrounded it with fake LED candles, and he is sitting in the middle of it. Waiting for me,

As I drift closer, I see a wine bottle and two glasses. There is also a plate of sandwiches. Brodie looks up at me and he is blushing. It's the most adorable thing I've ever seen. My heart is going to flutter right out of my chest.

"I'm afraid flipping pancakes and chopping veg is the extent of my culinary skills," he says, gesturing at the sandwiches.

I smile warmly at him. "I love sandwiches."

He grins back. The fake candlelight is reflected in his eyes, and I've never wanted to kiss anyone more.

I pull my gaze away to look over at Blue's pool. It's not lit, so the water is dark and still. It looks empty but I know Blue is hiding at the bottom somewhere.

"How is he?"

Brodie shrugs despondently. "I saw some ripples a moment ago and I think he popped his head up when my back was turned as I was laying the sandwiches out. I offered him one, but he disappeared."

I join Brodie on the blanket. "I don't think there is anymore we can do."

He sighs, "I think you are right."

His gaze meets mine briefly before darting away as if he is nervous. His hands fidget with a folded blanket beside him for a moment.

"I made you something. It's a bit cold out here and... you probably won't be allowed to wear it inside but I thought out here, just us. It will keep you warm and be a change."

He unfolds the soft blanket and holds it up so I can see the hole cut on it. He has made a poncho. I grin in delight as I take it and slip it over my head. It's soft and warm and it covers my midriff and best of all it's a pale cream color and not fucking red. I love it.

Brodie opens the bottle of wine and pours me a glass. Our fingers brush as he hands it to me and it's like touching electricity. My hand continues to tingle as I take a sip.

I look up at the sky. Through the orange glow of the city lights, only a handful of stars can be seen and some of them might be satellites. I sigh wistfully.

"I miss the stars," I say.

I look back down, and Brodie has leaned forward, and there are scant inches between our lips. I hold my breath in anticipation and sure enough, he closes the gap between us. The touch of his lips is feather soft and it takes my breath away. The kiss is gentle, coaxing, tender. The feel of it spreads throughout my entire body until every muscle is quivering. I want nothing more than to surrender to him completely. To drift away on a sea of bliss in his arms.

He yelps suddenly and pulls away. Confused and disorientated I look around but it takes me a moment to see that Blue's head is out of the water, right by us and his arm is outstretched with a firm grip on Brodie's leg. The mask covers most of his expression but the siren's eyes are glowing with a feral rage. The blue light of his eyes is fierce and unnerving.

"Don't move!" I hiss at Brodie without taking my eyes off Blue.

Shit. Any second now Blue is going to yank Brodie under with him and drown the human. By the time I run to get Lello and Ned to help it will be too late. Human's can't hold their breath for that long. And unlike Lello and Ned I need to breathe air too and I'm not strong enough to fight a siren on my own.

If only the bastard who hurt Blue had tried to take him on in Blue's own element, that would have been satisfying. But Brodie isn't the man who hurt him and Brodie isn't hurting me.

"Hey Blue, thank you for helping me, but it's okay," I try. "I want to kiss Brodie. I like him."

Blue stops glaring at Brodie to stare at me suspiciously but he keeps a firm grip of Brodie's leg.

"I really like Brodie. I want to mate with him. He is not making me do anything. I want to be his."

I'm pretty sure my cheeks are bright red right now but I can handle a little embarrassment if it saves Brodie's life. Though I can't look at Brodie, I just can't. I don't want to see his reaction to my words.

"Brodie is nice. He has been nice to you, hasn't he?" I add and I think I sound calm.

Blue stares at me and I hold his gaze evenly so he can see the truth of my words. Slowly his eyes fade to normal and then suddenly he is gone. Back under the water without so much as a ripple.

Brodie scrambles backwards until he is well out of reach of the pool, then he lets out a sigh of relief and his shoulders sag.

"Well, that's a good first date story, nearly murdered by a pissed off siren," he says wryly.

I laugh but I'm nearly exploding with light-headed giddiness. First date. Brodie said it was a first date.

If I get my way, it's going to be the first of many.

Chapter Twenty-Seven

Brodie

I'm sitting in bed, staring at this book but my mind is refusing to process the words. It only wants to think about that kiss with Red. Even the trauma of nearly being murdered afterwards is not a distraction. It wasn't our first kiss, but it was the most magical one so far.

That kiss was simply everything. I felt it in my soul. It blew away all the cobwebs in my mind, all the confused denial. It obliterated all the carefully constructed walls around my long cold heart. It enabled me to see clearly for the first time in forever and now I know the truth, with every fiber of my being. Red isn't just the most beautiful man I have ever seen. Red isn't just someone I have a crush on. He isn't someone I am falling for.

He is the one.

I never used to believe in soul mates and I'm not sure if I do now. I just know he is my special person. There will never be another. If I live for a thousand years, he'd still be the only one for me. I'm going to love him for eternity.

The thought should be terrifying. It should have me quaking with fear. Red has the power to destroy me. But I feel calm. Empowered even. At peace. I've found him and nothing will ever be bad again. He burns bright enough to chase away all the darkness.

My bedroom door opens. It's Red. My heart rate triples. He lingers in the doorway, a gorgeous flush on his cheeks and a nervous tremble in his hands.

"I... er thought we could continue what we started earlier?" he says.

Wordlessly, I throw back the covers to invite him in. Did he really think I would say no? Why is he so flustered? He is acting a million miles from the confident boy who walked into my med room on the day we met and asked to be jerked off.

Hopefully, he is just feeling overwhelmed by his emotions, and I can reassure him. Show him how much I worship, adore and cherish him. Let him know I am feeling everything he is and possibly more.

He glides over to the bed. Deftly strips off his clothes and slides in next to me. I send a quick prayer of thanks that I always get into bed naked, then I pull him close to me. The feel of his warm lithe body pressed up against my skin, makes me groan. I'm already in heaven and my cock is rapidly filling.

I stare into his eyes. They are sparkling with joy and he is smiling. His uncertainty has vanished, and that makes me happier than words can say.

I lean down and kiss him. The moment our lips touch, my soul ignites, burning brighter than it ever has before. It blazes and I have never felt more alive than at this moment. Red kisses me back with fervor, hunger and need. He wants me as much as I crave him and the knowledge of that makes me giddy with glee.

The kiss deepens, and he is pliant and yielding before me. Soft little moans are spilling out of his throat, each one is making my cock twitch. Each one is fanning the flames of my desire. I don't think I have ever been this aroused.

My hands roam over his body. I want to trace every part of him and memorize it, burn the knowledge of every plane and slope of his body into my soul so that I could sculpt him perfectly from memory. I already think I could. Even though I've never sculpted a thing in my life. If anyone could bring out the artist in me, it would be him.

Suddenly he is pushing me onto my back, the next thing I know, he is above me, straddling me. His gorgeous eyes dark with lust. I stare up at him in awe. I'm going to worship him forever.

His hand takes my cock and I groan. He lines me up with his slick drenched hole. He is wet for me. Just from our kiss. That is so incredibly hot.

He starts to sink onto me, his tight flesh enveloping my cock, sliding down inch by tantalizing inch. I groan and my head tilts back, I'm already seeing stars.

"Red!" I cry out.

"Jax," he gasps. "My name is Jax."

A jolt of intense pleasure shoots through me. He is trusting me with his name. A name he tells no one else. He has given me a secret part of himself.

"Jax!" I groan in delight as he seats himself fully onto me.

He whimpers and shudders. I think he enjoys hearing his true name on my lips. I'm going to keep it a secret between us. A name I only call him when we are alone.

A wave of sensation and pleasure washes over me, scattering all my thoughts. He moves above me, all graceful and sinuous as he rides my cock. It's a million times better than watching him dance. The sight is enticing. The feel of him gliding up and down my cock is incredible. I've never felt pleasure so intense. I never knew sex could be like this.

I watch him work, and I let the waves of bliss wash over me. His eyes are closed, his cheeks are flushed and his mouth is slightly parted. I could watch him seeking his satisfaction with me for eternity. I love that he is setting the tempo. Choosing the rhythm.

He picks up the pace and all my muscles tremble, I'm close, very close and he is too. His cock is very full, his ass is quivering around me.

Suddenly he opens his eyes and stares into my soul. I'm transfixed, pinned and hypnotized. He clenches around me and cries out. His eyes widen with the intensity of his orgasm and it allows me to see all of him. My peak hits me with the force of an atom bomb and I keep my eyes fixed on his as I ride the wave of overwhelming joy. I let him see all of me and nothing has ever felt more intimate.

He sags, so I grab his hips and lift him off of me and place him on the bed. We are both panting. I have never been happier. I think this is what ecstasy feels like.

I roll over and wrap my arms around him and hold him close. I don't know what the future has in store for us, but one thing is certain. I am never, ever letting him go.

Chapter Twenty-Eight

Red

I 'm chewing the end of the pen again. I huff in annoyance at myself and force myself to stop. My feet start to swing instead. Damn it, seems I can't think without fidgeting. At least I'm nearly done. I'm really dredging up ideas now and there is only one page left in this silly pink fluffy notebook.

I should be grateful that they gave me a notebook when I asked for one. It doesn't matter that it looks like something a seven-year-old would choose. And, actually the fact that it does, helps my cunning plan.

I just need to finish this blasted page. Filling this notebook has taken days and now the end is in sight, it's so frustrating. But I need to stay calm. I need to be able to think.

Suddenly inspiration strikes and the pen flies across the page. The ink soaks into the paper and in no time at all it's done. My thoughts have been captured and the notebook is filled. I want to do a little victory dance but there are cameras in my room.

I don't know who might be watching and I cannot arouse any suspicion.

But I cannot wait any longer either. I'm far too excited and impatient for that. So I scurry out of my door and head for the med room. I think Brodie is in there, it's a good place to start my search for him anyway.

I'm just making my way around the fountain when I nearly walk right into Ian.

"Where are you off to in such a hurry?" he asks.

"Just to find Brodie." My heart is hammering but I don't think Ian can hear it.

He grins. "Aww how sweet, you really can't get enough of his cock, can you?"

I bite my lip and say nothing. I don't want to antagonize him and I really don't want him to drag me off to prove his cock is better or bigger or whatever insecure or jealous shit runs through his head.

"What have you got there?" he asks, pointing to the pink fluffy notebook I have clutched to my chest.

"Noth... nothing," I stammer.

My blush is real and there is not a thing I can do about it, but I think it's going to help.

"Give it here," he says as he holds out his hand.

Slowly I move the notebook from my chest to his hand. He opens it and starts reading. I cringe and drop my gaze. Humiliation is burning through me. I'd probably be awful at writing love poetry at the best of times, but everything I know about Ritchie and the penthouse, disguised as declarations of love, has resulted in some truly awful verses.

Silence stretches for a long unbearable moment. Then Ian barks out a harsh laugh.

"This is quite something, Red."

He flicks through the pages, and I just want to wither and die. I don't think Ian is smart enough to find the hidden meaning, and he definitely doesn't think I'm clever enough to hide anything, but it's still nerve-wracking. Ian reading my soppy heartfelt feelings is intrusive enough on its own. While the words and phrases I had to use are awkward and forced, the feelings behind them are genuine. And I don't like Ian seeing them. It feels like he is sullying them. As well as seeing far too much of my innermost thoughts.

He slams the book shut and thrusts it back at me. I hug it to my chest.

"I'll give you some free advice, Red. Don't give this to him. You are just a nice hole he likes to fuck. Trust me. The novelty of a self-lubing ass will wear off soon enough and he will move onto one of the others."

I grimace and stare at the floor. He is wrong, so very wrong. I know it, but damn if it doesn't speak to the deepest darkest self-doubts in my heart and I hate Ian for it. I don't want to awaken my insecurities. Brodie loves me and I love him. I just want to exist in that glorious bubble.

He laughs again and strolls past me. Freeing me to go on my way. Except now my mood has soured. Glumly I walk the rest of the way to the med room.

Brodie is here, and my heart does a little skip at seeing him. My good mood makes a tentative return. His wonderful scent drifts over to me and I want to inhale it. My inner wolf wants me to rub myself all over Brodie to bathe in his smell and imbue it into my own skin. Thankfully, I manage to resist. I don't think Brodie is ready for full on shifter behavior yet.

He looks up, sees me, and smiles. A beaming smile that lights up his eyes and sets butterflies fluttering in my belly.

"I have something for you!" I exclaim as I thrust the ridiculous looking notebook at him.

He raises an eyebrow and walks up to me. He places a hand on the notebook and I have to prise my fingers off to relinquish it to him. He takes it and opens it. I swallow and watch transfixed as a flush spreads across his cheeks as he reads.

Oh god, please let him be clever enough to see my hidden meaning. Please, please don't let him think I've just handed him a book of cheesy, awful poetry. There are even a few lines in there that wax lyrical about the beauty of his cock. I will literally die of embarrassment if he doesn't catch on.

Okay, I'm going to leave, because standing here is torture. I turn around but suddenly his hand is on my wrist. I look back over my shoulder at him. His eyes are bright, gleaming and intense.

"Thank you for this," he says. "It means a lot," he pauses, "to me."

My heart goes crazy and my head spins with glee. He understands. He has seen there is a hidden meaning in all the poems. It is going to help. I feel the biggest smile of my life spread across my face. Brodie beams back at me in return.

"You're welcome," I say softly.

He releases my wrist and I skip off. Everything is going to be okay. I just know it is. It's just a matter of time and then everything is going to change. There is a whole bright new future waiting for me, one with Brodie in it. I can't wait.

Chapter Twenty-Nine

Brodie

This book Red has given me is an absolute gold mine. I've already read it cover to cover several times and gone up to the roof terrace for a smoke, to transmit all the new information to the Council. But I can't resist reading it again, just in case there is anything that I have missed. Sometimes my mind slips out of decoding mode and just reads the soppy and sometimes downright filthy words and I feel myself blush. It would be heavenly if Red did feel this passionately about me. Maybe he does?

The lights flash above my head. Smithson is here. Damn it.

Carefully, I put the notebook away. Should I go lurk in my usual corner? Should I observe who Smithson and his guests pick? What if he chooses Red? A wave of nausea washes over me.

It's not like me standing there watching helps anyone and I really don't want to raise any suspicion, not this late in the game when the end is in sight.

But my feet seem to be taking me to my lurking corner anyway. Oh well, it's a habit of mine now. I don't think anyone will think anything of it.

Lello dashes past me in the hallway, he is running towards the front door, not the stage. I guess Smithson hasn't visited for a while and the poor kid can't contain his excitement.

Sure enough, as soon as Smithson walks in with a large entourage, Lello pounces with a squeal of delight. Smithson catches him easily and he grins.

"Hey baby. You are looking as pretty as ever. Are you feeling better now?"

"Yes Daddy!" exclaims Lello happily but I hear a note of sadness in his voice.

Shit, this is the first time Smithson has visited since Lello was beaten up. It seems even that neglect hasn't cured the kelpie's addiction. Or has it? There is something about Lello's behavior that I can't put my finger on, but it makes me wonder if he is starting to doubt, if not fully come to his senses about Smithson. But there is no time to ponder that now.

I hurry up the hallway to the party area before anyone notices me and questions my presence. I'm just in time to see Blue make his way to the stage, his head is down and my heart breaks for him. The other boys move around him and do their best to hide him with their own bodies.

Smithson's entourage swarms in and spreads out. He has brought staff with him too and they hurry over to the bar and start preparing drinks.

"Ritchie's Rainbow!" boasts Smithson.

His guests make suitably impressed noises and congratulate him. Smithson visibly swells from the praise. Sick fuck. I really have never hated anyone more.

Quiet jazz music starts to spill out from the hidden speakers. Drinks are served and Smithson's party gets settled on the plush sofas.

"Nick, you can choose first. Which boy do you want to have for the evening?"

A heavy set middle-aged man licks his lips. "I'm not even gay, but fuck it, they are so pretty!"

Everyone laughs and the sound coils around my gut until I think I'm going to be sick.

"The one in green," says Nick.

Jade quickly hides his grimace, then he steps off the stage and joins Nick on the sofa.

"Steve, you can choose next," says Smithson magnanimously.

"Yes!" says, presumably Steve, as he fist bumps the air.

Everyone laughs again. Steve looks around and grins, clearly lapping up the attention. He looks like a dumb tech bro. Probably someone who went to school with Smithson.

He stands up and makes a big show of considering the boys on the stage. "The one at the back, Blue."

There is an audible thud as Blue backs up and hits the wall. Even from here I can see how wide his eyes are and how much he is trembling. One of the other boys gasps in horror.

"Actually, I don't think Blue is well enough," I say as I step forward.

Smithson whips around in his seat to glare at me. "He is physically damaged?"

"No," I confess reluctantly. "But he is traumatized emotionally."

Smithson gives a snort laugh and turns back around. "I don't have time for snowflake sensibilities," he declares before gesturing at Ian. "Bring Blue to Steve. Use the taser if you have to."

"No Daddy, please!" begs Lello wide eyed as he tugs at Smithson's shirt.

A loud smack fills the air. It takes me a moment to process that Smithson has dealt Lello a vicious backhander, and the kelpie is now crumpled on the floor, holding his cheek.

"I don't come here to be disrespected! I work damn hard to keep you all in luxury and I deserve to relax!" snarls Smithson.

The room falls eerily silent. The tension is palpable. Red steps off of the stage into the silence. He sways up to Smithson with the best seductive walk I have ever seen.

"You are right Ritchie," he breathes huskily. "We are all sorry."

Smithson shoulders relax and he takes another sip of his drink. Has it worked? Has Red managed to diffuse the situation?

"Fine," snaps Smithson. "Red, you make Steve a happy man."

My heart clenches and I can't breathe. I swear being run through with a javelin would hurt less. My vision is swimming, my fists are clenching. Part of me is screaming to take action, to do something, anything. Another part is demanding calm, demanding that I don't throw everything away in one pointless, reckless move. The two parts of me are fighting savagely. Tearing chunks out of each other while I stand here completely immobile.

"And Ian can remind Blue of his place. On the stage. So we can all watch the show."

My gaze snaps to Ian, but the overseer doesn't look at me. Or anyone. He just starts walking towards the stage whilst unclipping the taser at his hip.

My horrified gaze lands on Ned and I see he is staring at me intently. As is Red. Slowly my gaze tracks around the room. Lello is staring at me too, from his place on the floor whilst clutching his cheek.

Five pairs of eyes are fixed on me, waiting, hoping. Five powerful paranormal beings and me, against these humans. My mind frantically tries to calculate the odds. Pink, bless him, isn't going to be much help. But Ned will be formidable. As will Red. Kelpie's can be damn vicious too. If Lello does actually side with us against his beloved Daddy.

I don't know how well Jade can fight but if Blue stops cowering and realizes what's going on, that will more than make up for any lack of ferociousness on Jade's part.

Can I get to Gray's room and free him? Or would he just disembowel us all?

Have I read Ned's expression correctly? Is he really willing to tear these bastards to shreds? What about his grandkids?

As I'm thinking, Ian reaches the stage and Blue drops into a ball with his hands above his head.

Fuck this shit.

I press the tiny, discreet button in my pocket. I have no idea if the Council will help. They do nothing that is not methodically planned, but fuck it, it's worth a shot.

Then I nod at the boys, and all hell breaks loose.

Chapter Thirty

Brodie

The world is chaos and noise and motion. I so desperately want to look for Red and the other boys but I know I have to concentrate on the fight in front of me, my own assailant. Getting myself killed because I am distracted will be no use to anyone, except for our enemies.

I knock out the man who was stupidly trying to face me. These men are all soft. Rich, spoiled business men. They don't know how to fight. They have probably never been in a fight before. This is going to be easy.

I glance over to Blue, when all of this kicked off, Ian was standing over him with a taser. The siren is the only one facing an opponent with a weapon. But when I look over, Ian has his back plastered to the wall, the taser lax in his hands and he is staring wide-eyed at the fight with Blue unharmed next to him.

I have one moment of dizzying excitement, thinking it is going to be so easy. But then the armed security guards run in. Fuck.

I rush the nearest one and topple him to the floor before he has even had a chance to get his bearings. As I wrestle him the skin on my back prickles. I'm acutely aware of how exposed I am, of how easily one of his friends can shoot me in the back. But the bullet doesn't come. I guess that means my friends are whooping his friends' butts. That is so good to know.

"Stop!" yells Smithson and something in his voice makes me turn to face him.

He is standing in the middle of the room. His face is all bloody and bruised, but he has an arm around Pink's neck and one of the security guards' guns pressed to the boy's temple.

The room falls silent and still. I glance quickly around to assess the situation. Red looks unharmed, as do the others. Some of the humans are out cold but I don't think any of them are dead.

I can't see any of the other guns anywhere but none of the humans have them. The boys were successful in getting the weapons away from the goons. I wish they had kept them though, but then I realize with a jolt that it is unlikely any of them know how to fire one.

My gaze flicks up to the stage. There is still one potentially armed foe. Ian and his taser are still pressed against the wall. But Blue is no longer on the stage, he is standing close to one of the security guards. It looks like the siren was brave enough to join the fight. I'm proud of him. Snapping out of a PTSD episode to engage in combat is no mean feat.

We are still screwed though. No one can get to Pink. The realization is awful as it slowly sinks in. It's over. We are done for.

I'm enraged that Smithson has won. There really is no justice in the world. The last shred of belief in any deity or a benevolent universe, turns into ash within me and I can taste the bitterness on my tongue. How can it be over, just like that?

"Lock the boys in their rooms," orders Smithson.

Slowly, his remaining conscious goons start to move. I can see the future unfolding in front of me. The boys are going to be locked up. Punished awfully and then have what little freedom they had curtailed. Their lives are going to be a thousand times worse than they were before. Red's life is going to get worse. He is going to suffer.

And I'm going to get the shit beaten out of me and then I'm going to be killed. But I don't give a fuck about that. I'm full of rage at myself. I was supposed to free these boys, free Red. Make their lives better, not worse. I have failed them all in the worst possible way. Red most of all.

My gaze locks with Pink, to try to reassure him, but instead my heart freezes and time screeches to a halt. Sheer horror replaces the blood in my veins. No, no, no. I try to move my body, I try to step towards him but it feels like gravity has increased a hundredfold. It's like trying to swim through treacle.

As I struggle, Pink moves. He gave up on life long ago. He doesn't care if he dies. I've known that since the moment I met him. And now I can see it in his eyes as clear as day, he is not even thinking of it as a sacrifice. To his mind, he is merely escaping in a different way from his friends.

His elbow moves and jabs right into Smithson's stomach. I watch in slow motion as the billionaire starts to fold in half. The gun goes off and Pink falls to the floor.

I roar, and suddenly time unfreezes, and I can move again. I launch myself into an attack on the bastards around me. No fucking way am I letting Pink's sacrifice be in vain. I really hope the other boys also seize this moment and resume the fight.

My world narrows to the next kick, the next punch, the next opponent. Grunts and groans are the only sounds.

"Freeze motherfucker!" snarls Smithson.

I look up from my crouch to find his gun inches from my forehead. Shit. No one has been able to disarm him. I haven't heard anymore gunshots so hopefully no one else has been hurt. It's just my turn to die.

I glare up at him with all my rage and hatred. Can I take him before he puts a bullet in my brain pan? It's got to be worth a shot.

Suddenly slender hands appear on either side of his head. Then with a deafening snap his head is twisted violently to the side, far further than a human head is able to turn. His lifeless body crashes to the floor like a sack of bricks. Revealing Red. The omega has a very determined look on his face.

Fuck yeah! Red just used his shifter strength to snap Smithson's neck. I've never been so proud and ecstatic in my life.

My vision swims, and my hearing distorts. I sway. Shit. I vaguely recall getting a sharp kick to the head at some point in the fight. I hope it's just concussion and not a brain bleed.

Red drops to his knees in front of me. He holds my shoulders to steady me. He looks so worried it makes my heart flutter. He really does care for me.

Dimly I hear an explosion. Shouting. The sound of running feet. Oh fuck, reinforcements. I need to get to my feet. When did I fall to my knees?

The newcomers rush in and recognition washes over me. Council. The Council are here. They came. Better late than never. Red is safe now. All the boys are. I can pass out now. So I do.

The blackness is peaceful. But I can't wait to wake up because I have a feeling I'm going to be in Red's arms when I do. And that sounds like heaven.

Chapter Thirty-One

Six weeks later

Jax

The lamb casserole smells perfect, but I can't resist having a little peek. This kitchen is a joy to work in and I love it. Though truth be told, I'd probably love it if it was a hovel. It's the kitchen of my home. My home I share with Brodie and the boys. It symbolizes both my freedom and my future.

I'm just closing the oven door when Brodie's arms snake around me from behind. I smile and lean back into his embrace. He keeps his arms around my waist and I adore the feeling of being held. It still feels strange that his arms are touching the fabric of my tee shirt and not my bare midriff. Six weeks later and I can't get used to wearing proper clothes. The joy they give me is immense though. Simple jeans and tee shirts feel like such a privilege. One day I might work up to something fancier.

"How is Benji?" I ask. My mind still thinks of him as Pink, but I don't let my tongue slip up.

"He's good, he is going to come eat with everyone in the dining room."

My heart does a little skip of joy. When I checked on him this afternoon, he was merely thinking about it. It pains me to see how slow his recovery is. I know humans are weak and that getting shot in the head is no small matter, but he has had the best magic healers, and then Brodie taking care of him, and yet he is still so weak. It terrifies me to think that Brodie is just as vulnerable. Those two hours he was unconscious after the fight were the worst two hours of my life. Even though everyone was reassuring me that he was going to be fine.

It's something that I just can't bear to think about. So I drag my thoughts onto a different topic.

"And Lello, I mean Doolin?"

Damn it. Getting used to everyone's true names is hard. Hopefully, they will all continue to forgive me when I slip up, just as I don't mind when they call me Red.

Brodie sighs sadly and releases me from his embrace. I whirl around to face him.

"Not so good. He is fading a little more every day."

I swear inwardly. Kelpie mate bonds are strong. Bonded kelpies rarely survive the death of their mate. I'm still furious that Doolin's people won't help him or have anything to do with him. Damn them and their puritanical monogamous views on sex. It's hardly as if Doolin chose any of what happened to him.

"We really need to find someone to mate him?" I ask despondently even though I already know the answer.

Brodie nods and we stare at each other sadly. How the hell are the Council going to find someone? Someone ruthless enough to force a new mating bite on Doolin, but then not take advantage of having the little kelpie utterly devoted to him for forever?

"And we need to find someone to empty Benji regularly," I say. "And someone to feed Gray."

The awfulness of it all weighs heavily on my shoulders. Poor Gray, I'm not even sure he knows he is out of the penthouse. He certainly hasn't been with it enough to tell us his name.

"And Rue needs the ocean but other sirens might attack him because they'll think he is weak."

Brodie pulls me to him again and tucks my head under his chin.

"It's going to be fine. It will all work out," he says.

"Ned already is hardly here, always going to check on his grandkids. And Jade... Sithri is frantically applying for jobs. Our family is already falling apart," I whine.

Brodie hugs me tighter. "No it's not. Sithri just wants some normalcy, he has said nothing about moving out. Ned is never going to abandon Doolin, or you or the others. He can't exactly stroll into his grandkids life and say who he is, the best he can do is stalk from a distance."

His words do make me feel better.

"And we will find good men for Doolin, Benji and Gray. And we will find a way to keep Rue safe from other sirens. You've all survived the worst. These are the good times now."

I sigh. "You are right."

He steps back from me and gives me a cheeky grin. "I know, I'm always right."

I chuckle. "I'm not so sure about that."

"I know I'm right about it being time to dish up dinner," he teases.

I give him a playful whack on the shoulder and turn back to the oven. As I dish up dinner, Brodie goes and rounds everybody up. The wide double doors to the dining room allow me to watch it fill up. Fill with people and noise and good natured bickering. Just like a pack. Because it is a pack. My pack.

Sithri and Rue come and help carry all the plates through. I put bread and drinks on the table earlier, so we are all set. Everyone tucks in and I feel a burst of pride at their murmurs of thanks and appreciation. I love that they all like my cooking.

I look around my found family and I feel happy, despite my worries for the future. Benji and Doolin both look pale but they are both smiling. Freedom looks good on them. Brodie is right, everything is going to be okay. The Council are doing all that they can to help us. They gave us this beautiful house, complete with security guards. They have given each of us a generous allowance for the rest of our lives. And they will find the men that Doolin, Gray and Benji need. Just like they will find a way to keep Rue safe in the ocean.

I glance at Brodie sitting by my side. At least they don't need to find me an alpha. I've found my man, or he found me. Whichever it was. And him being human isn't a problem at all. He certainly knows how to take care of me during my heats. I flush at the most recent memories from a week ago. I'm sure the entire house heard me, but it can't be helped.

Maybe once my heats have settled into a regular cycle, Brodie and I can slope away for a couple of days when I'm due. But I don't even care if my cycle never settles. Brodie is right here, and he isn't going anywhere. He will always help me whenever and with whatever I need. I've never been more sure of anything. He is everything that I need.

As if we have a mate bond, and he can read my mind, he takes my hand under the table and gives it a squeeze. I squeeze him back as happiness flutters through me. I think it is finally sinking in. It's over. I'm free. My chains are gone. I'm finally an unfettered omega.

The End

The boys' real names

Red – Jax

Lello – Doolin

Pink – Benji

Jade – Sithri

Blue – Rue

Ned – Ned!

Gray – He hasn't told them yet

Thank You

Thank you for reading my book, I hope you enjoyed it!

Please vote for which boy's book you want me to write next!

https://www.srodman.net/the-unfettered-series.html

Want more Red & Brodie?

How about a FREE exclusive bonus epilogue, where they get away for a dirty weekend when Red/Jax goes into heat?

Tap the link to sign up to my monthly newsletter for instant access!

https://www.srodman.net/newsletter-sign-up.html

If you are already a subscriber, don't worry! The link was in the 22nd April 2023 newsletter.
(If you signed up after that date, follow the link in your welcome email.)

Limited time offer **Not one, but TWO free books when you sign up!**
Sign up now and your welcome email will contain links not only for the bonus epilogue but also for a free copy of Incubus Broken and Omega Alone.

If none of that takes your fancy, how about exclusive short stories and opportunities to receive free copies of new books before they are released?

Sign up here.

https://www.srodman.net/newsletter-sign-up.html

It comes out once a month, you can unsubscribe at any time and I never spam, because we all hate spam.

If the link is broken please scan the QR code below or type www.srodman.net into your brower.

Books By S. Rodman

Books By S. Rodman

For an up to date list, you can view my Amazon Author page
HERE
Or view at www.srodman.net

Darkstar Pack

Evil Omega

Evilest Omega

Evil Overlord Omega

Duty & Magic: MM Modern Day Regency

Lord Garrington's Vessel

Earl Hathbury's Vessel

The Bodyguard's Vessel

Duke Sothbridge's Vessel

Non Series

All Rail the King

Shipped: A Hollywood Gay Romance

Hunted By The Omega

Hell Broken

Past Life Lover

How to Romance an Incubus

Lost & Loved

Dark Mage Chained

Prison Mated

Incubus Broken

Omega Alone

Evil Omega

Also by S. Rodman

Gay. Necromancer. Werewolf. Supervillain.
Power bottom.

Silas is all of these and more.

Silas Northstar is an outcast. A wolf shifter without a pack. A hated and feared necromancer, infamous for killing an entire pack. He aspires to become the true supervillain people whisper he is.

He is also an omega. Heat cycles are a fact of life, but he has no problem finding casual fun with humans to satisfy his needs. He can't imagine that ever changing. He doesn't do lonely, and he definitely doesn't do feelings. He doesn't need an alpha.

Dean Westlake is a happy-go-lucky alpha who is trying his best to settle into his new pack in a new city. The pack's Alpha, George, is an idiot, but Dean is glad to not be alone anymore. Few packs will accept a second alpha, so he knows his choices are limited. He needs to make this work.

The rumors of the city's supervillain sound far-fetched. He's not worried.

Then the Westlake pack captures Silas. That night he goes into heat. Someone has to deal with it.

Dean gets the honor, and the fireworks begin.

The morning light shows Silas has vanished. Everyones says no one can keep Silas Northstar for long.

Dean vows to prove them wrong.

getbook.at/EvilOmega

Lord Garrington's Vessel

Also by S. Rodman

It's 2022. Magic isn't supposed to be real. Arranged marriages aren't supposed to exist.
How are gay arranged marriages for the purpose of magic a thing?

Fen has grown up all alone in boarding schools. Never meeting any of his family. At his graduation, his older brother turns up to take him home. Except Fen discovers he is the result of a shameful affair and not actually related to Lord Garrington at all. Yet, for appearance's sake, everyone must continue to believe they are brothers.

To make matters worse, an indiscretion reveals that Fen is a vessel. Someone who grows magic but cannot wield it. Magic can only escape his body and not kill him by regularly submitting his body to a mage. Hence the crazy arranged marriage idea. It's a shame the only mage he wants is his arrogant and obnoxious fake brother.

Lord Xander Garrington, like all British nobility, is secretly a mage.

He was only supposed to pay the boy off, but Fen turned out to be outrageously pretty. Then he turns out to be a vessel. The opportunity is too great to miss.

He needs to pretend Fen is his brother and sell his stepmother's bastard to the highest bidder. Securing the best possible match to advance the family's fortunes.

If only Xander's emotions would obey.

He is supposed to sell his fake brother, not fall for him.

getbook.at/LordGarringtonsVessel

Dark Mage Chained

Also by S. Rodman

When Max is asked to guard a sexy dark mage, he just knows it isn't going to end well.

Max is a light mage who likes his own company and living alone in his ramshackle cottage.

The prisoner reeks of disgusting dark magic, is hot as hell and a sarky pain in the ass.

He's also dangerously full of magic. Max needs to empty him and the only way to do that is through intimacy. Simple enough.

No need for emotions to get involved.

Atticus is used to being passed around. He's not used to the way Max looks at him. It's annoying and stirs feelings in him. He will just have to escape as soon as possible by any means necessary.

There is no way he is going to catch feelings.

There are only two things Max and Atticus agree on. Love at first sight is not real and enemies to lovers is not a thing.

viewbook.at/DarkMageChained

S. RODMAN

Prison Mated

Also by S. Rodman

Alpha Logan has been in a human prison for years, hiding his shifter identity. One day he smells an omega and his world comes crashing down.

Humans don't believe the paranormal world is real and everyone wants to keep it that way.

But omegas are gorgeous, sexy as sin and their pheromones attract humans.

An omega in a prison full of pent up violent men is a disaster. How can Logan keep him safe without revealing his paranormal strength and betraying their kin?

What if he falls for little omega and starts to believe keeping him safe is more important than keeping the paranormal world hidden?

Feth believes he is a terrible omega. He is beyond relief when a hot alpha finds him and offers him protection. But pretty soon he messes that up too. Surviving prison seems easier than working things out with his new alpha. Will the alpha like him? Claim him?

Will he get prison mated?

viewbook.at/PrisonMated

Past Life Lover

Also by S. Rodman

Who knew putting the bins out could be life changing?

Sam is cleaning up his bar after closing time when out of nowhere a beautiful man jumps literally into his arms and won't let go.

He soon discovers that the gorgeous stranger, Tally, has had a very traumatic night.

So all this talk of them being together in a past life and Tally escaping from hell to be with him again, must just be trauma induced delusions.

It has to be? Right?

There is no way this cute femboy is a reincarnated dark lord.

But Sam doesn't mind looking after Tally until he feels better.

It's not like the poor young man has anywhere else to go.

It's not like one good deed will lead to his life being turned upside down and inside out. Will it?

So what if strange things start to happen? Such as hell hounds and then Lucifer's husband showing up.

Tally might just well be worth it. Tally might just be worth everything.

Coming 14th July 2022

Pre-order now getbook.at/PastLifeLover

Earl Hathbury's Vessel

After years of cruelty, how do you learn to trust? To love?

It may be 2022, but the modern world has done nothing to protect me.

I live in the world of the British nobility, a secret society of magic, mages and vessels.

There are strict rules and customs and no freedom at all.

My name is Charlie, but to society, I'm just a vessel. A person who grows and absorbs magic within them, but cannot wield it.

As tradition dictates, on my eighteenth birthday, I was given to a mage. From that day onwards, every seven days for four long years, Earl Rathbone took my body to take my magic.

Earl Rathbone was a cruel and harsh master. But it was 'the done thing' and society turned a blind eye to my mistreatment.

Until the earl's son finally intervened and whisked me away.

Sending me to Archie. The Earl of Hathbury.

Archie is kind and sweet. The man loves books nearly as much as I do. He is nothing like Earl Rathbone.

Yet, giving Archie my body and my magic is daunting. But it is my duty and a necessity. As a vessel, I need a mage to regularly empty me or I could die.

To my great relief, Archie is understanding and gentle, and it's not long before I start to fall for him. Finding my duty more of a pleasure.

Archie seems to enjoy our time together more than is proper, and I am hopeful.

But can Archie be trusted? Is he really safe? Will I ever be truly free?

Available August 14th 2022

viewbook.at/EarlHathburysVessel